Kill 'Em with Kindness

By C.S. DeWildt

Copyright © 2015, C.S. DeWildt

All rights reserved. No part of this electronic book may be reproduced or transmitted in any form or by electronic or mechanical means including photocopying, recording, or by any information storage and retrieval system, without the written permission of the publisher, except where permitted by law.

This book is a work of fiction. Names, characters, places, and incidents either are the products of the author's imagination or are used fictitiously, and any resemblance to actual events or persons, living or dead, is entirely coincidental.

Published by Mike Monson and Chris Rhatigan
Edited by Rob Pierce and Chris Rhatigan
Cover design by Eric Beetner

For Sarah, Toby, and Ben

One

IT TOOK NICK a moment to recognize her when she hobbled into Nate's place, and when he did he felt sick. He didn't know her, not personally. She was a few years younger than Nick, and he thought maybe their time at Horton High School had overlapped, but he *did* recognize her from the bar. She was a regular, and she was Chad Toll's girl. Her name was Kimmy Flynn, and by anyone's regard she was beautiful. A real fucking knockout. Most days.

Nick took her in with his beer as he tipped back his glass. Her face was purple on the right side. One eyelid stretched across her face, sealed tight and so swollen it looked like the slightest poke would burst it like an angry boil. Her right arm was in a sling and she moved with a limp, trying to hide it and failing.

But the most striking thing, aside from her not being with Chad, was the metal halo screwed into her head. She walked only as far as the first barstool, lifted herself gingerly and sat with a pained sigh. Nate continued wiping a spotless glass behind the bar as he and Nick watched her pull a pack of Marlboros from her jacket pocket, reaching across herself with her good arm. She lit one with care, took a long first drag. The long cigarette matched her legs, which despite the rest of her, were perfect as they wrapped around the legs of her barstool, a creeping vine of smooth flesh.

"Gonna get her a drink?" Nick said. Nate twitched out of his frozen state, shuffled sideways to the bottles that lined the mirrored wall behind the bar. Nate was old and twisted with the reminder of his childhood polio, but he moved without hesitation. He didn't ask her what she wanted, just mixed her the usual screwdriver and put it in front of her. Nate stepped away then returned to her with a red swizzle straw as an afterthought.

"Thanks," she said.

Nick tried to focus on the ESPN Classic hockey game, the Wings and the Avalanche from back in 1996, but he kept hearing his mother's voice telling him not to stare. Kimmy had been big-city beautiful, beyond the small pond of a town like Horton. Now she was a mess of bruises and swollen skin and metal. But her new face couldn't take away from how Nick remembered her, coming into the bar on the arm of the lug, Chad, certainly the one who'd messed her up. Chad was king in Horton and Nick knew no one else who'd dare love her that way. Nick inhaled; she smelled like honey and antiseptic. Her gasps between long held breaths drew his attention as Russianimport Steve Yzerman glided on the frozen water of the Joe Louis Arena, transported across not only space but time, landing in front of them on the small screen of the old television atop the refrigerator.

"Fuck yeah!" she shouted as the Wings went up 3-2. She winced as Nate put another screwdriver in front of her. She sucked down the drink and Nick watched her smile into the bar. "I fucking love that man," she said quietly.

When the final buzzer announced the end of regulation, the Red Wings of the past had again spanked the Av 7-3 and Nick swelled with Kimmy's happiness. His wife had been a fan of the Wings. A long time ago.

But any joy Kimmy had inside was knocked out of her again as the door opened and the bowling league regulars stomped in from the cold rain. It was early August but a freak cold front had moved in and brought a freezing rain that made it feel more like February, the brutal wind-whipping tail of the Horton winter. Each time the door opened it was the same. Nick watched Kimmy attempt to turn her head, wincing against the pull of the screws in her skull, too drunk to stop herself until finally the door opened and Chad Toll stomped in, his crew and his canines in tow. The dogs were massive beasts, loyal, drooling Caucasian Mountain Dogs that went with him everywhere, black as the night and each of them easily over two hundred pounds. The men flanking him were less intimidating; bean pole Erik Babin and farm-dirty Russell Potter. But they were with Chad and that made them dangerous.

Nick watched Kimmy open her mouth to speak but the words stopped cold as she noticed the pretty young blonde thing holding Chad's hand, a petite sprite of a girl initially hidden behind Chad's frame. The girl was the only one to acknowledge Kimmy, giving her a self-satisfied smirk and dismissing her completely. Chad looked past Kimmy and nodded to Nate behind the bar.

"Beer for her," he said, thumbing to the blonde. Chad's gaze glanced over Nick as he led his cutie to the pool tables in back. Nate drew two High Lifes, left the bar to deliver the drinks. Chad Toll was the only person that could pull Nate from behind the bar. If anyone else, even the guys in his crew, had expected Nate to play waitress they'd get nothing more than a "fuck you." But Chad was taken care of. Always.

Nick watched Kimmy watch Chad and his new girl in the reflection behind the bar. Her face betrayed no jealousy or anger. The only clue she felt anything was the hard shake of her hand as she swirled her fresh drink, adding the clink of ice on glass to the cackling mix of warming voices and music and clicking billiard balls.

Chad played a few games of pool, spoke loudly. Nick listened; Chad's league team, the T-Birds, had rolled their way into the seasonal semi-final round. The girl with him laughed donkey loud at everything that came out of his mouth, joke or not. The blonde had her own crew in tow, a redhead and a brunette, both bar pretty, rough skin and wrinkles under their pancake foundation. Kimmy set her drink down hard on the bar and Nate was as quick to replace it as she was to drink it.

Chad led Erik and Russell and the dogs away from the pool tables. The blonde girl attempted to drape herself on him, looking for Kimmy's eye, but Chad dismissed her with a single hand and without a word, left her to stare at Kimmy before she slunk back to the pool table.

The crew of men and dogs stopped behind Nick, close enough that if they weren't trying to intimidate him they either didn't know he was there or found him inconsequential. As if to emphasize that point, one of the dogs lifted a leg on the feet of Nick's stool.

"Gimme the Maker's," Chad said. Nate grabbed the half full fifth of whiskey from the bar. "Nah. The unopened bottle." Nate retrieved the new bottle without a word and Chad twisted the waxy red cap and tossed it to the bar, spraying the clean surface with tiny drops of whiskey that looked like spittle. Chad brought the bottle to his lips and opened a shadow-hidden door in the corner just beyond Nick's seat at the end of the bar. The men and dogs descended into the basement, Russell Potter closing the door behind himself, making the door disappear into the shadows again, never even there.

The bar was quieter after they'd gone, as if the jovial atmosphere was nothing more than a show for their collective benefit. More likely Chad had taken the mood with him, like the whiskey, like Kimmy's beautiful face, like everything else he wanted.

At the pool tables, the blonde who'd come in with Chad was talking to her girls, laughing, speaking quietly but loudly punctuating her secrets with "bitch" and "whore" and "skeez" and "slut." Nick watched Kimmy in the mirror then watched with her as she stared at the reflected trio, their laughing and tossing of hair for the crowd of men swooping in. Nick watched the heavily mascaraed eyes at the pool table, how they found her with each dirty word uttered. He watched as Kimmy's reflection slid off the stool, drink in hand. She moved as smoothly as the alcohol allowed, having traded her pained limp for the top-heavy, swooning sway of five screwdrivers. The bar went quiet and the buzz and prying eyes of the table outshone and out-hummed the bare fluorescent bulbs hanging high on the arched ceiling.

"What the fuck you want?" the redheaded girl said as Kimmy approached. The redhead stepped in front of her. "Love your hat, cunt!" Nick held his breath as Kimmy seemed to shrink before him, and he felt for her, beaten, bruised, and now berated. He felt sorry for her, wanted to help her slip into one of the cracks in the wooden floor.

Nick soon found his pity misplaced as the broken girl swung her good arm and smashed the glass against the side of the girl's head, sending the redhead to the floor screaming and bleeding. She scooped up the cue ball from the table in a precise swipe, then set herself on the true target. The blonde's eyes grew large and she put up her hands in a show of dovelike surrender. But her submission was futile as Kimmy's next strike crushed the bridge of her nose, the wet crunch like footsteps in firm snow.

The brunette backed away as Kimmy pulled her bad arm from the sling and grabbed a handful of blonde hair before slamming the billiard ball into her face, again and again. The blonde cried, *begged* the crowd for help until a smashed nose, missing teeth, and a mouthful of blood forbade it. She went to her knees but Kimmy wouldn't relent, just kept beating her and when the girl finally dropped, Kimmy fell with the pull of the dead weight and straddled her, smashing the bloody blonde into unconsciousness and beyond. Less the hoots and cheers, no one spoke. No one tried to help the girl on the floor.

Nick didn't remember the journey, his mind seeming to come back to him only at his arrival on the scene, catching up with his body only after he'd grabbed Kimmy by the sleeve, pulling her easily from the broken mess on the floor. She didn't fight him. She didn't cry. She let herself be led away to a chorus of "boos" and "let 'em fight." Nick led Kimmy out the door.

Outside the rain still fell, the cold wind whipping up tiny droplets that stung like bees.

"I want to talk to Chad," Kimmy slurred. "I want to talk to him. I want to talk to that FUCKER!"

"You got to go. Police will be here. You want to spend the night in jail?"

"I don't give a FUCK!" Kimmy screamed, but she barely resisted as Nick ushered her to the passenger side of the purple VW. Her silence was her concession as Nick fished inside her jacket pocket for the keys. He raised the fob over his head and pressed the unlock button over and over until her car's tail lights flashed. Nick opened the Cabriolet's door and helped her into the passenger seat. He shut her inside the car and listened to the rain, waited for the sound of sirens. He looked back at Nate's, wondering if anyone had followed them. The bar sat silent but for the muffled music of the jukebox.

Nick found an address on her ID and drove Kimmy Marie Flynn to her place at 1905 Beech Street, Number Two. He drove slowly, the VW's bald tires spinning to a start, fighting the ice for traction. A bit unnerving, and the last thing he wanted to do was wreck Chad Toll's girl's car, but the tiny burg of Horton, population 5,706, was especially dead this time of night and Nick didn't see another car.

Nick found Beech and made the turn. Kimmy had been asleep, but Nick looked over and she was awake now and looking at him, turned to her side and hugging a knee.

"The Wings win?" she asked quietly.

"Yep," he said, and started looking for 1905.

"Good," she said. She closed her eyes and whispered, "Thanks. But you don't know what you did now."

"Oh, what did I do?" Nick laughed lightly.

But she didn't go on. As they pulled into the drive she said, "How's he going to make me burn it? He wanted me to tell him 'no.'"

Nick helped her up the steps to the door of the apartment house.

"I got it," she said, fumbling with the keys then dropping them in the grass. Nick grabbed them, shook off the wet and unlocked the door for her as she held his shoulder for balance.

Kimmy stumbled into a narrow foyer and Nick followed her to the dark apartment at the end of the hall. He unlocked the door and she entered, disappearing into one of the rooms. Nick waited a beat, tossed the keys inside onto the little table stacked with mail and a child's artwork, handprints in fingerpaint. Another table further down the long foyer was knocked to the floor, a hole in the drywall about the right size for Kimmy's skull. A fleeting glimpse into another dark room showed nothing but further disarray. The entire place smelled as if something had rotted in the trash while Kimmy was in the hospital.

Nick continued to listen for a moment before locking her in and shaking the handle. He threw on the hood of his old tan parka and hit the street. The rain was slowing, but the air still cut through Nick's layers. Since he was on foot, he wished for the long cold of true winter. A good freeze would cut Nick's trip time in half, allowing him access to the onion and celery fields too soft to cross other seasons of the year. The only ones with that ability were the migrant Mexicans who passed through with the season and the crop. So Nick skirted the cumbersome fields in favor of the road. He tightened his hood against the wind but couldn't keep out the smell of onions.

Nick reached his house and only when the warmth of his home overwhelmed him did he realize he was exhausted. He wanted nothing but to kick off his boots and fall hard into oblivion, a good place to lay low.

He traced his fingers over a series of photos that lined the long hall to the master bedroom. The affection soured and his fingers pulled the frames from the wall with such a nimble perfection, it almost seemed as if that's all they'd been made for, or perhaps the pictures fell from his caress, repelled by his touch. They were mostly photos of Grete and him. Domestic shit he no longer wanted but didn't have the energy to part with.

Nick hit the bed but didn't fall away from anything. Instead he found himself in a dark place like the one he'd come home to nearly five years ago when Grete had shut herself in the garage. Then he could see and he was with her in the Mustang, the Boss Shelby, same model her dad owned, shut away in the warm dark garage. Nick sat still and watched Grete slump over the steering wheel. He knew, in his dream logic, that he could open the door, save her, but he didn't. Instead he waited to die. But he didn't. He waited. And waited. Finally, confused by the fumes in the car, he tried the door and found it locked.

Knowing he was trapped, he began to panic. He kicked the glass, knocking dead Grete to her side. Between her legs he could see their baby, a prematurely expelled stillborn monster, troll-like and hissing. The thing looked at Nick and began moving toward him, climbing onto the seat from the floorboards. Nick kicked and kicked and kicked the glass. The thing moved closer. It spoke to him.

"You killed her," it said. "You killed her. You were never enough for anyone."

Nick continued to kick, frantically, a scream poised to jump from his lips, kicking the glass. Kicking the glass. Kicking. He woke with a start, legs still fighting the sheet. Nick lay still and though he knew it was a dream, the feeling that he was with his dead wife and monster child was slow to recede. He remained motionless until sleep grabbed him again and delivered him into the true blackness Nick wanted.

The dream wasn't new. He'd had it nearly every night for the first six months. Then it receded to just once a month. And now barely ever...but this was twice in a week.

In his dark sleep he couldn't care and, upon waking, he would remember it differently, an altered detail, possibly imagined, but branded into his memory as truth: It wasn't Grete with him, but

Kimmy Flynn in the car. No monster baby. Only Kimmy.

Two

NICK WASN'T EVEN sure what day it was, let alone the time, when the knocking woke him.

"Nick!" someone called from outside. "Nicholas! Wake up! I know you're here."

Nick rolled over and sat up, rubbing his eyes and pulling on his pants as the knocking continued. "Nicholas!"

"What? What!" Nick said as he opened the door. He knocked his knuckles on top of the man's head. "Hobo! Hobo! Hobo!" Nick put a hand up and squinted into the sun, relenting to its heat. "What? What?" The man named Hobo stepped back and covered his head.

"Asshole!" He cracked a smile, "Where were you last night?"

"Nate's, where do you think?"

"You forget I was coming by last night?"

Nick stepped aside and let Hobo in. "It's Saturday. You always come on Saturday."

"I told you last week I had to come by on Friday. My wife's fucking sister's thing? Said I'd come by on Friday. I left you a voice mail."

"Huh. I never check that thing."

Hobo sighed. "Can I just have it? Please?"

"All right, all right, all business," Nick said.

"I had a guy set to take it last night. He doesn't like to wait."

"All right. Calm down. You're here. I got it." Nick cocked his head toward the kitchen. "C'mon."

Hobo looked down the dark hall as he passed, glancing over the photo frames littering the carpet. "Your pictures are all fucked," he said.

***

Nick led Hobo through the kitchen and down to the basement, a cluttered mess of Grete's old clothes and all kinds of baby shower gifts: boxes and bags and gift baskets, still wrapped in paper and seven years of dust. Nick had tossed it all down the stairs at a time when he'd desperately needed it gone. Hobo had long stopped asking if he was ever going to clean it up.

The men waded through the plush and plastic mire to a door at the base of the staircase and passed through into an unfinished yet pristine concrete shell of a room, warmer than the upstairs. In the corner a humidifier rumbled low. Combined with the heat it was like entering a swamp. Nick took a seat at a long workbench and began working the dial of a combo lock securing the large red safe. Hobo eyed the only other door in the room, dark varnished teak wood secured with three dead bolts that led into an unpainted five-by-five-foot drywall closet.

"Can I have a look?" Hobo said. "You mind?"

Nick glanced up, nodded to the silver key hanging on the wall adjacent, went back to the combination lock. "Knock yourself out."

Hobo opened the door and the light inside the closet was warm and white. "Oh, look at these beauties," Hobo said.

Nick smiled despite himself. He loved plants. All plants. "Should be ready to cut and dry next week."

Hobo silently admired the cannabis, sixteen plants on a series of shelves that lined the closet's interior. Each shelf held pots with varying stages of growth. The tallest plants on the floor, buds nearly ready to cut and dry. Younger plants sat on the shelf above. On top were the smallest, maturing sprouts. Hobo pulled one from the top shelf and admired it before gazing at the rest with the same look of lust. "Forget about thumbs; you're green to the shoulder."

Nick pulled three one-pound bricks of marijuana from the safe's guts, each brick wrapped in heavy, industrial cellophane, the same kind he'd wrapped the Chancellor's car in after being expelled from State.

"Who says a college education isn't valuable?"

Nick said. "Now close the door, huh? You're fucking with the light."

Hobo reached high and placed the small plant back on the top shelf. Nick cringed as he envisioned Hobo dropping the pot to the concrete. Then he saw Hobo's belt line as his jacket raised with his arms, saw the pistol tucked there.

"Since when do you carry a piece?"

Hobo turned, looked confused a few seconds. "Oh, yeah. Lately. Open carry. Easiest way to break the law. And you know, safety? Never really know what people might be carrying."

"Aren't your customers like eleven years old?" Nick said. It was an old joke. Back in college Hobo had nearly gotten busted dealing at a middle school near campus. He was there to sell to one of the teachers on the guy's lunch break, but campus security came around and chased him off, literally. He nearly got caught, but hopped the chain link fence surrounding the campus and found a slow-moving freight train just beyond the school property. But the thing picked up speed and Hobo was nearly to Chicago before the train slowed enough to hop off, find a phone, and call Nick to get him. The story even made the local paper, no names, but it got around campus and pretty soon Jonathan Prince was known only as Hobo.

Nick didn't get such a close call when the campus police kicked in his door six months later. No nickname either.

"Who's your new guy?" Nick asked, almost as an afterthought.

"Huh?"

"Whoever wants the pound? The reason you're knocking on my door at seven o'clock in the morning."

Hobo stalled, but finally said, "Chad Toll."

"Give it back." Nick reached for the cellophane packages. "I'm serious."

"You can't make me do that."

"Can't I? I saw his girl at Nate's last night and she had her head kicked in pretty fucking good. Jesus, man! Chad Toll?"

Hobo sat there, looking shamed but complacently so, defeated but alive. He shrugged.

Nick stood. He wanted to throttle Hobo. Nick had managed to do okay with the business. A few thousand a month, just to survive, not draw attention. Hobo then broke up the bulk and turned it into whatever he turned it into. Nick didn't usually ask questions, but in this case he was glad he did. Or maybe not. Now Hobo was in with Chad Toll, so whatever he was making, it would never be enough.

"You've got no fucking sense. 'Under the radar'

was rule number one from day one."

Hobo didn't speak. Instead he tossed a wad of bills to Nick, who grabbed it from the air, technically completing the deal. Nick looked at the money, then at Hobo. What was he going to do? Leave the guy dry? Even if he didn't feel some loyalty to the dummy, holding out meant that Chad and his crew would come sniffing around.

"You shouldn't have done it," Nick said.

"He came to me, Nick. And when you're in with him you're in with him. Or you're out, permanent. He made that very clear. So there you go."

"How long you been dealing with him?"

Hobo looked away. "Six months."

Nick shook his head. "Unbelievable. What else you keeping from me?"

"He wants to double his order."

"Oh, this just keeps getting better."

"And he wants to meet you."

"Oh Christ."

***

Nick watched out the kitchen window as his friend left. The sun was high and bright and ice melt from last night's frozen rain fell from the roof like a second shower, exclusively over Nick.

Hobo gave him a wave through the water and glass. They'd been together a long time, a serendipitous meeting due to nothing other than a random roommate assignment. Never friends, just each with a skill set: Nick knew the plants and Hobo had a network of customers. From the very beginning it was little more than a professional partnership. When Nick was kicked out of school they kept going, Nick growing out of his parents' basement and then his own apartment. The business took off with Nick's newfound free time. Nick continued studying horticulture at the community college and the business grew with the addition of his own new contacts. Then the golf course came calling. And Grete. Then the law. And darkness. The garage. More darkness.

And what had been a tolerable stagnation of body and soul was about to become something new. It was easy to think that with a little luck, the something new would work out and everything would be okay. Easy to think if you were a fucking moron.

Three

NICK SAT ALONE on his end bar stool, sipping a Killian's and smoking. The TV was on. This year's state championship featuring the Horton Hawks had finished the same way as last year, with an out-of-sync Horton destroyed by the defending champs from Ypsilanti. They shouldn't have been there, the Hawks. Their schedule was weak, they were nothing more than the cherry on top of the crap sundae. But they showed up and the only bright spot on the team, quarterback Tre Brickle, had been taken out by a brutal helmet strike to the knee. The kid rolled on the field, crying and writhing in agony to the sound of cheering Ypsi fans. As soon as he was off the field the game was on with number two QB, hot-shit sophomore Grady Jenkins. The boy managed to keep his joints intact, but he was swallowed by the dominant Ypsi defensive line over and over. And the screen at Nate's showed it all, showed the new number one lose his lust for the game. A single game it took to beat it out of him. You could see it in his eyes with every shot he took downfield, with every yard lost to his inefficient scramble from the shadows of boys who were more dangerous than most men.

The city limits sign on the forty-five east of Zeeland boasted last year's team as District Regional Champs. Runner-up State Champs. Those signs were intended to inspire community pride, but in Horton's case, it was nothing but a sore reminder to those men commuting back into town from their jobs at the clock or furniture factories near the lake. And of course, any informed outsider could snicker, because even they knew the real winner of that game was the Hawks coaching staff and various boosters who'd taken bets.

But no one was asking. And when the door opened at five o'clock and Chad Toll walked in with his dogs and his boys, Nick knew that some very slippery questions was about to be asked of him. And when Chad stopped behind him and grabbed him by the shoulder—not friendly, not aggressive—Nick was sure of it.

"Want to see the conference room?" Chad said. Nick followed the man and the dogs to the basement while Russell and Erik hung back and played pool.

The conference room was low ceilinged and carpeted in thick black and orange shag from the last decorator forty years ago. Chad had a seat at the poker table and pointed for Nick to sit across from him. A stained glass lamp hung from a chain over the center of the table, throwing a warm yellow glow and a mix of red, blue and green stains onto the white ceiling.

"You showed up on my radar twice in one night."

"Sorry?" Nick said.

Chad shook his head and gave a sad smile. "Don't. Don't be a dipshit. I've got enough dipshits. I know what I need to know about you. All but your reasons. You drove Kimmy home," Chad said. "Why? You fuck her?"

Nick shifted, hoped it looked like he was seeking comfort, not words. "No. No. She wasn't in shape to drive. And I didn't want to see her get taken in for beating on that girl."

Chad nodded as if he understood, but he narrowed his eyes. "Fuck you care?"

Nick shrugged. "I should have let her be, maybe. Or not. I don't like to get involved. Usually."

"But you did. Twice. We have a mutual friend?"

"Yeah. Business partner. But look. I mean it, I took her home and dropped her off, yeah, that's it. And I didn't know Hobo was working with you until this morning. He never told me."

Chad said nothing, just searched Nick's eyes for deception. Despite his desire to remain calm, Nick's shifting took on a weasel's squirm.

"She was upset," Nick continued, grasping. "I

didn't want to see her locked up. That other girl okay?"

Chad shrugged, scratched the head of his right-hand dog. "No need to worry about that." Satisfied with whatever he found in Nick's gaze, Chad grabbed a loose cigarette from the poker table, lit it, blew a long stream of smoke into the twirling ceiling fan. Nick watched the smoke diffuse into a thin cloud that vanished except for the lingering smell.

"You believe in fate?"

Nick shook his head, confused then annoyed. "No, I guess I don't."

Chad eyed him and Nick again felt the need to speak. "You? Believe in it?"

"You bet. And the more I hear out of your mouth the more I believe in it." Chad tipped back what was left of the bottle from the previous evening. "Nate told me you were a farm boy."

"I guess," Nick said. "One of Pop's entrepreneurial pursuits. Raised pigs for about a year. Tried breeding horses. Didn't pan out."

"He drink?"

Nick nodded.

"He beat on you?"

Nick shifted in his seat. "When I deserved it."

Chad laughed. "I always deserved it." He took another long drag and blew the smoke, shaking his head, dismissing a memory, and letting the fan clear it away. He crushed out the butt in the full ashtray in front of him. "You know anything about cows?"

"A little. Took some AG classes at State."

"College boy."

"A year. Then a couple semesters at Ottawa Community."

"Why'd you quit?"

Nick shifted forward, just barely. "That's my business."

Chad grinned. "Yep. There it is." His smile fell. "You're your own man. I can respect that. I am too. You don't have to *tell* anything. Here's what I know: You were kicked out for dealing marijuana in your dorm. Lost your job at the golf course for the same reason. Don't you learn? Ha. Is that what set your wife off? Financial strain? I mean, a lot of folks got money problems, so maybe that was just the final push. And being so close to the edge."

The dogs knew how to read the slightest threat against their master. Chad smiled again as Nick glared and the two-hundred-fifty-pound beasts at his side rumbled.

"Don't be mad, Nick. Lots of folks got problems. Not like yours maybe. But their own. And whatever they are, to those people, they're the most important problems in the world.

"But I can help you, Nick. That's why I'm asking about you. I don't like to see a useful man go to waste. You like jerky?"

Nick minded the eyes of the dogs, nodded, "Sure."

Chad reached into his pocket and pulled out a small plastic bag of beef jerky. He tossed it across the table.

"My dogs love it," Chad said, scratching both of their heads. He looked Nick in the eye. "Feed them," said Chad. "Hand to mouth."

"It was a ride. That's it." He was stalling, he knew damn well what had happened: Chad didn't get his package and talked to Hobo. Hobo probably sitting in the same chair Nick was sitting in now. Nick had known Hobo a long time. His kind of criminals were pothead middle school teachers and gas station employees and college kids. Hobo had a kid, a wife. He'd give up everything with barely a squeeze.

Chad was becoming impatient. "Don't worry about that. I know people, many people, two of which are these dogs that will tear your ass up if I say so. Nothing recognizable left if you're stupid enough to be thinking about it. Now feed these dogs."

Nick saw little choice but to feed the beasts the jerky.

"Go get it," Chad said. The dogs moved quickly

and stood in front of Nick. They took the meat from his hand, both growling on verge of bite until Nick withdrew his mitt. Chad smiled. "They only bite people who need to be bit."

"Nice to know," Nick said.

"Who needs to be bit is who I say."

Nick nodded. Part of the program. For now.

"You're the grower. Small time or I would have heard of you before now."

"I get by. It's just me, but you know all that."

Chad nodded, his good 'ol boy smile returned. "Look, Nick, here's what's happening. I'm going to sell your weed for you. Maybe. There's a couple things have to happen first. You do right and I can protect your enterprise. Make it more profitable. Better than 'getting by.'"

Nick looked at the dogs, placated for the moment by food and calm. Nick tossed two more strips of jerky on the floor.

"Doesn't seem like I have much of a choice."

Chad smirked. "There's always a choice, Nick. Don't fool yourself. You got a choice. You always got one." Chad stood from his chair. "You make your choice by morning. I hate to rush a man through his chance to choose. So go. Use your time. I got churches to burn."

The expression was new to him, but he'd been let

go and Nick didn't need to be told twice. He stood, backed halfway to the door. The dogs stood alert, rumbling just barely as Nick turned away and moved past the Kiss pinball machine and small private bar and the freedom of the door and stairwell. Nick took one last look back to see the dogs returning to their master.

When Nick stepped back into the bar it was shut down tight, dark. Erik and Russell were still at the table but they put their cues down and made for the basement when they saw Chad had released Nick.

The Horton PD squad car was there in the parking lot waiting for him, engine running, red brake lights lighting up the exhaust like blood. Chief stepped out. A big fucker. Nick remembered him from one other run-in. A speeding citation that included a chat about his record. "I like to know what's what," he'd said before taking a twenty off Nick and letting him go with a warning.

"What's this?" Nick asked.

"Nick, are you going to make me go through the entire speech of what and why? Or are you going to get in this car? You can save us time by letting me tell the story on the way." Chief rubbed his thumb and forefinger on the end of his sheathed baton. Turning and pinching it like a whore's nipple. Nick felt as if he were being given another choice.

"Just tell me what for. And I'll come along."

Chief spat on the ground. "What it's about ain't worth a sack of sand here, Nick. But if you need to know, right now it's about not getting your head caved in."

Nick looked over his shoulder. He felt the opposite of being watched, felt he was actively avoided, as if no one wanted the burden of bearing witness. If Horton had a single strength, it was looking the other way.

Chief opened the door of the cruiser. "So come on now. Let's go. You can ride in back."

Four

NICK SAT WITH both hands cuffed to the chair. Chief sat across from him, the surface of his desk lost beneath a mound of paperwork. Chief put a small digital recorder on top of a stack of manila folders.

"Time you drop Kimmy Flynn off?"

Nick shrugged as he gathered his thoughts. "One maybe?"

"Maybe?"

"I think it was one o'clock. Nate's was still open."

Chief nodded and grabbed a bottle from the desk drawer. It was a fresh fifth of Hennessey whiskey. Chief opened the bottle and took a long swallow. He offered Nick the bottle and Nick shook his hands in response, the clanking metal logic enough for Chief to withdraw the offer. The big man tipped the bottle back, drained a quarter of the whiskey before stopping to catch his breath.

He took another long drink. "Daddy's juice," Chief said to no one. "Time you leave her?"

"Saw her inside and left. I don't really know. I made it home just after two, so I guess it was right around one, like I said."

"Walk home?"

"Yeah. What's this about? She okay?"

"I don't know. She look okay to you?" Chief said.

"Beat to shit by somebody," Nick said.

"Car wreck, night before last. She claims." Chief smiled. "Her car look wrecked to you?"

Nick shook his head.

"I'm not worried about the night before last though. I want to know about last night. You know what happened though, right?"

"I don't," Nick said.

"Don't what?"

"Know what this is about." Nick shook his hands, rattling the metal cuffs against the chair. "Is this necessary? How about taking these fucking cuffs off?"

"You like rape?"

"Hell you talking about?"

"You like rape? Yes or no?"

"No."

"Ha. So you consider it more of a chore?"

Nick shook his head, exasperated by the game Chief was playing. "I don't like rape and I didn't rape anyone." He shook his hands against the cuffs again.

Chief kept smiling as he pulled opened the laptop on his desk and spun the computer around. The screen was littered with various documents and file folders, much like the analog desktop in front of him. The video player window came to life and Nick watched. He saw Kimmy sitting in the same chair he was in now. She was crying. She wasn't in cuffs.

"He brought me home. I thought it was, I didn't know what to think. I didn't even realize who it was until it was happening." The sobbing girl on-screen lost it, sobbing into her tissue before reining it in enough to go on. "I was so fucking out of it. I thought he was just being friendly. Ha. Friendly. Who needs friends, right?" She let out a flat laugh and sniffled into the tissue. "He opened the door for me. I was pretty out of it, but I remember I dropped the keys and he opened the door for me. I didn't even hear him follow me in. Then I was on my back. I told him no, but he laughed and said 'this is happening. Best just go along for the ride.'"

"And then what did he do?" Chief's voice said, tinny and off-screen.

Real Chief nodded from behind the laptop, looked at Nick with an amused grin. "You like this show?"

"He raped me," Kimmy said. "He slapped me around a little, then Nick Gillis raped me."

Off-screen Chief asked another question. "You know him? Before he offered you a ride?"

"Seen him in the bar," she sniffed, then no further answer but crying. And it was convincing. You could almost see her in that hallway while Nick put his fists to her, his boots, his cock.

Chief came around the back of the desk and blocked the view of the monitor with his giant frame as he closed the laptop. "So there we are," he said. He grinned and showed Nick the shining silver handcuff key.

"I didn't do it. That girl is lying."

Chief didn't seem to hear him. "Let's find you a bed," the big man said.

***

Nick spent the rest of twenty-four hours in a holding cell before Chief freed him and pushed him out the front door of the station with no explanation. He didn't need to give one. Nick saw clearly as Chad's black jacked-up Ford truck rumbled idly on the opposite side of the street.

As Nick descended the station house stairs to the sidewalk, the tinted window lowered.

Chad flashed a shit-eating grin, stuck his head out the window.

"Choices, huh? Ha!"

Five

NICK BRACED HIMSELF in the bed of the truck as Chad took sharp corners on gravel roads. Inside the cab were Chad, Erik, Russell, and the dogs. Acne-pocked Erik looked out the back window, laughing as he watched Nick bounce and slide. Nick wedged himself against the gate and the side, sure to spill out into the country night should the tailgate give. He tried not to think about that as he watched the dust fly up red behind them in the taillights.

Chad drove south out of town and cut east into the small borough of Jessup, an unincorporated village of about fifteen hundred people. Up ahead, the red flash of every county emergency unit within ten miles was easily overpowered by the sun. Chad slowed as they approached.

"Damn shame," Nick heard Russell say as the truck slowed and weaved around the scene, through a front yard, and honked to clear a crowd of gawkers. Many of the onlookers were crying as their church burned to the ground. The heat and light lapped at them like a tongue.

"Damn shame it didn't happen when it was

supposed to," Erik said.

Nick caught Chad's eye in the rearview. "Everything happens for a reason," Chad said. "We've got ourselves a bona fide expert with us tonight!"

They continued east in the truck, picking up speed as the smooth rural pave job cleared ahead of them, a straight shot to nothing. Nick lost his ball cap in an eighty-mile-per-hour wind gust and watched as it shrunk into the darkness, gone. He eyed a screwdriver wedged in the grooves of the bed liner near his feet. Usually he'd have a blade in his boot but Chief had neglected to return it with the rest of his personals, or had lifted it for himself. It was a nice blade, double action switch and sharp as hell. And as tempting as the screwdriver was, it wouldn't be much use against the three men and the dogs.

Chad's truck came to a hard sliding stop in front of the Porter Farm sign. Painted below the name was a black and white milk cow, crude but quaint.

"Out," Chad said over his shoulder. Nick climbed from the back of the truck while Chad, Russell, and the dogs jumped out of the cab. Erik slid over in the front seat and took Chad's place behind the wheel. He drove off back the way they came, leaving them to the country quiet.

Nick followed the remaining men and beasts. No

one spoke. The only sound was the soft patter of secret footsteps. Even the dogs seemed to control the force of their gait, slinking softly on giant paws.

Past the house, each of them crawled through the horizontal beams of a metal gate. It was painted white and glossy smooth and the porch light from the back of the house was reflected down the entire length of its reach. Beyond the gate was a two-track farm road and another gate, this one a wooden interruption in the miles of electrified wire that surrounded fifty acres of Porter farmland. And over that fence and into the graze land, cows and the smell of manure. Nick soon realized that avoiding the piles of shit in the dark was a futile pursuit. They walked through the herd, quiet except for the wet slosh of shoes in shit. Deeper into the herd they bumped cows out of the way, some of whom complied while others stood stupidly wondering nothing, impossible to move.

"Tell me what you learned in vet school," Chad said.

"Wasn't vet school. Agriculture."

"You ever feel for a calf?"

"No," Nick said.

Chad stopped dead and his hounds turned and flanked him at the ready. He gave Nick his empty eye again, the one that could either smile or bite.

"I've seen it done, though," Nick said.

Chad smiled. "Good enough for me!" Russell joined in his laughter and tossed Nick a large container of petroleum jelly. And before he could mount a protest, pointless as it might be, Nick found himself up to his shoulder in cow snatch.

"Ever read McMurtry?" Chad asked. "Last Picture Show?"

"No," Nick choked. He didn't feel like discussing literature. "I don't feel anything up here."

"It's alright. One of 'em is bound to be carrying," Chad said. "Book was weird to me," he continued. "Like how nonchalant these farm boys were about raping a cow, taking turns holding it down and swapping out so each one gets his sloppy seconds. Or thirds. It's weird, right?"

Nick thought the whole fucking thing here was weird. "Yeah," he said. "It's pretty weird. But maybe not if you're a farmer. Ag frat at State got suspended my first year there. They were making their pledges assfuck a goat." Nick gagged on the smell of cow taint. "Jesus Christ, there isn't anything up there." Nick pulled his arm hard against the sucking slurp of the cow's twat. It came free and he stumbled back, hit the ground and fell into a steaming pile of fresh shit. More laughter as Nick got to his feet. He followed as they looked for another candidate.

"He said they'd be fat," Chad said.

"They all look fat," Nick said, holding his breath.

"Erik probably does have a better eye for it, the specific condition we need."

"Why isn't he here then?"

"Because he's at the pickup, and he didn't want to stick his arm inside a cow tonight." Chad pointed to a fat animal with a large black spot that looked like the state of Florida. "That one."

Again Nick slid his petroleum jellied arm inside the cow's vaginal cavity and up through the cervix to fumble and feel for a calf. The pressure stimulated the colon and a fresh load of manure was dumped steaming over his shoulder.

"All right," Nick said in a voice that betrayed his desire to puke. "Fucking finally. Yes. There is a calf in here."

"Good enough," Chad said. "Get yourself out of there or I'm going to think you like it."

Chad threw a loop of rope around the cow's neck and it followed without much trouble. Nick did the same as the cow, stinking just the same, pulled by his own invisible lead. They walked for a long time in silence and every sound of the bucolic night came to sing songs of babbling water and crickets and horny leopard frogs. The air was a sweet and sour mix of honeysuckle and cow taint as Nick's soggy arm burned cold in the cooling night.

Russell snipped the wire fence at the end of the property and the crew stepped into a creek bed. They followed the flow further south, splashing in the shallow water. Nick looked up through the tangled nest of thin branches that sliced apart the sky and moon overhead. He listened to the footsteps. After a time everyone fell into rhythm, predictable and hypnotic.

They reached the cement tunnel that ran the creek underneath Twenty-Fourth Ave, and as the men and beasts began to climb the bank up to the road, the lights of the waiting truck flamed alive. Nick raised a hand to his brow and looked under the light as Erik appeared in front of the vehicle and stood waiting for the lead at the top of the hill.

"Fire out?" Chad called from below.

"Ha. Nah. They'll be tied up all night I'm sure."

At the back of the truck was a long grated metal ramp. The cow moved well until it hit the metal incline, then its cloven hooves recoiled as if the ramp were on fire. The men pulled, each grabbing a handful of the heifer and forcing her. She began to grunt and whine, stamping her feet and snorting. She calmed herself as the men loosened their grip and soon stood still, unbothered. Unbothered until the men expected her to take that first step onto the ramp again.

"The slope up the creek bed is steeper than this!"

Russell pulled hard on the rope. "Anybody got a fucking club? Beat this bitch up there." Russell looked around. "For real, find me a hammer or something. Get the tire iron out of the truck."

"That isn't going to work," Nick heard himself say. His voice was slightly mocking. "She doesn't know what the hell this is. Only knows grass and dirt, not metal."

"So what the fuck should we do, Farmer Cunt? You gonna stick your hand back up there, make her go that way?" Erik chuckled, but Chad was silent, waited for Nick to show how much he really knew.

"Got a blade?" Nick asked. One of them had to. He'd feel better if he had it in his hand. Russell and Erik looked to Chad. Chad pulled his knife from his pocket and tossed it to Nick, who snapped it open and used the sharp tip to put a hole in the shoulder of his shirt. He stretched the hole with his finger until it ripped and he pulled the sleeve free. "Ruined anyway," he said as the rest looked on. Even the dogs seemed curious.

Nick draped the sleeves over the cow's eyes.

"That's not going to do shit," Russell said. "She can't even see it."

"He's right," Chad said. "That Claire Danes movie said the same thing. That one where she's that retarded farmer. What's her name, Nick?"

"Temple Grandin."

Chad nodded and smiled Nick's way. His proud smile slipped away as his gaze found his lesser children. "You idiots know that?"

"Let's fucking see if it works before you start slinging the hurtfuls," Russell said.

Blind, she went up the ramp peacefully, without incident. Chad drove more carefully than before, now that he was toting a thirteen-hundred-pound pregnant heifer in the back of his truck. Nick didn't have to worry about being thrown out at high speeds any longer, but the cow shat and farted continuously, making him wonder which was preferable. Probably the cow. He was covered in shit already anyway.

Nick sat in the remains of the filth he'd landed in and tried to look from the outside in on his new situation. He cursed Hobo silently, but it did little to absolve him from his share of responsibility. He'd interfered. If he'd only let Kimmy beat that girl to death with the cue ball. If he'd been home when Hobo came by, he'd still be within the safety of his ignorance. But none of that was the case. And now he was here, waiting for whatever was next.

Chad turned south out of gravel and onto the smooth, fresh pavement of Riley Road. The truck picked up speed. The road dipped over a long chain of hills and Nick felt his stomach float with every drop. The stop signs they flew past were nothing but blood-red warnings to be ignored.

Nick looked over his shoulder, watched the road flee beneath them. They were miles away from the church, but the sky above it still burned bright for the Lord, lit the sky as purple as a screaming bruise.

***

The stolen flatboat ferry floated slowly down the Grand River. The cow stood still in the center of the barge. At its front hooves was a large plastic tub full of grass and straw. The cow chewed and looked around easily, as if this event was the most normal thing in the world. The dogs sat calmly behind Chad, who stood at the bow, watching the night. Erik was playing with his phone at the stern, while Russell sat in the captain's chair, piloting the boat.

"Let's talk a bit, Nick."

Nick stepped to the bow and joined Chad. The dogs looked intently at Nick but didn't stir. Chad lit a cigarette and offered the pack to Nick. Nick took one of the cigarettes and lit it off Chad's waiting lighter.

"You know Kimmy? I mean, before you drove her home."

"No. I've seen her in Nate's and all. But no. I never knew her before."

"She was in a sad way before she met me. She's a beauty, right? I mean, when her face isn't all beat to shit, she's a looker, yeah? Say 'no' you're either a fag or a fag liar."

"She's a pretty girl."

"Shit. Pretty. Girl's a fucking knockout." There was a chuckle at the back of the boat. Chad turned, smiled. "You like that, Erik?" He faced out over the water again. "So you didn't know her but you gave her a ride. You do that a lot?"

"No."

"So why her?" Chad said.

Nick wasn't sure why. Or what Chad expected him to say. "I didn't want to see her get in a wreck. Or kill somebody. I lost my wife a while back."

"Smoking the exhaust pipe, right?"

Nick looked out over the black water, wished there were more to see.

Chad smiled at Nick, as if he took joy in needling him. "Lost my old man the same way," Chad said. "Not the car. Hung himself in the woods behind out house. Law on his heels. I'm the one who found him."

Nick looked at Chad, but Chad was looking out over the water. He no longer wore the satisfied grin. "Scary how quick you can get over something like that."

Nick remained silent but he didn't deny it. He

remembered the relief that had been mixed up in his grief, the feeling he'd tried to deny was there. But it had been and eventually Nick realized that the relief was all that had been there. Hard as it was to admit, his new life was just something to get used to, like an unfamiliar car or a set of clothes that needed to be worn in. One day they felt a part of you. And when they did feel a part of you, it was as if they'd never felt any other way.

"Easy for me to say," Chad said, pulling a tall boy Miller from his jacket pocket. He handed it to Nick and retrieved another for himself. "My old man was a miserable prick. Drunk. Mean." He cracked his beer and took a long pull. "But you lost a kid."

Nick nodded. "I did."

They sat in silence. Chad drained his can and tossed it into the river. "We used to have goats when I was a kid. My dad had a friend and they dealt some weed. They were tight. I'd have called him Uncle Jim if he'd been the type. One night I go down to the barn because I had to feed the goats. They were little pygmy things. They were nice enough but I didn't have a use for them. But I had to feed them and I'd forgotten and I had to go out late. It was dark and the light was on in the little barn shed where we kept the goats at night. The light was always on so I didn't think anything. But when I went in I saw Jim with his dick in the female of our pair. He—Ha!—He's wearing this pair of muck boots went up to his thighs, and he's got this poor goat's back legs in the boots with his, holding her still and steady while he got her, got her *goatie* style I guess." Chad stopped talking and grabbed another beer from the foam cooler on the deck behind them, tossed one to Nick.

"I was dumbstruck," Chad said. "And Jim doesn't see me right away but he feels me and he turns toward me, still stuck with the goat and this goat is licking its black eyes. And you know what it looked like? Its face? Like it was the most normal thing in the world. And Jim is looking at me and then past me and his face melts from this look of, I don't know, *transcendent satisfaction*, and I'm saying it fell away to a look of horror. I thought the look was for me, for me finding him there, but I felt a hand on my shoulder. It was Dad.

'You see this, Chad? You see what this man is doing?'

I nodded and Jim was trying to get himself out of the goat. 'Don't let up on our account,' Dad says. And he points his .38 at Jim and says, 'C'mon, finish up. Least you owe my boy is a full show. You're fucking his goat.' But by then of course the mood had been ruined and Jim just started crying and dropped the goat, just let it hang and bahhhh from the shared boots.

'Please don't kill me, Chuck,' the guy says. 'I got kids.'

Dad laughs and says, 'Interesting choice of words.' Then he looks at me. 'You can't let a man fuck your goat. It's not that he's fucking it, some men just can't help themselves. It's that the goat he's fucking is yours.'"

Chad tipped back the last of the beer and Nick watched his profile in the green moonlight. Chad tossed the empty can into the river. "This is what happens when you fuck a man's goat: the man is put down. And the goat too because while innocent victim maybe, ruined is fucking ruined, right?"

Nick had no answer for that so he helped himself to another beer. "Where we taking the cow?" Nick asked.

"Down river," was all Chad said.

***

They met the truck north of Grand Rapids at the northernmost tip of Cascade County. The transfer happened in the middle of the river. Russell let up on the throttle and the air fell to a cold quiet with only the sound of torn water as the boat glided, then a piercing splash as Erik threw out the anchor. Chad tossed a rope to one of the two dark figures on shore, then both of them pulled the boat to the launch. On the west bank behind them sat the ass-end of a slow-moving truck, a twelve-by-eight-foot box. The brake lights lit up the exhaust. Nick wondered where the cow was going but knew it was foolish to ask.

The men didn't exchange words and the cow gave no trouble—followed the pull of the lead and clumped its hooves from the metallic deck to the grooved concrete that rose from the water. One of the men on shore led the cow into the truck and the other tossed a fat manila envelope into Chad's waiting hands. Chad, in turn, handed it to Erik, and Russell cranked the diesel motor.

"Make yourself useful," Chad said. "Raise the anchor."

Nick pulled the rope and Russell immediately throttled the rumbling diesel, still heading north. Nick caught a last glimpse of the truck, the cow being led up the ramp. If his geography was right, there was nothing close but the Redi-Farm facility; they owned everything around here.

"Erik," Chad said. "Money." Erik tore open the envelope, counted out four small bundles, and set them next to Russell, on the dashboard above the flickering gauges. Russell knocked a fist atop the small pile and the gauges woke fully for a moment before flickering again.

Erik took several more bundles, looked to Chad, and handed them to Nick. Nick thumbed the bills and stuffed them in his jacket.

"Seems a good rate for raising an anchor."

Erik chuckled and turned away to the water.

"Maybe," Chad said. "But we got one more stop tonight. Then we'll see how you feel about your pay."

Erik laughed again and Russell joined in, now thumbing through his own cut of the deal.

Nick felt uneasy but figured the cash in his jacket meant some kind of security for him. So far he was chauffeur to Kimmy, cattle probe, anchor raiser, and soon to be something else. He looked at the dogs, lying on the deck with rested bodies and ready eyes.

Russell steered starboard and killed the engine. He brought the boat into shore too fast and jolted everyone loose.

"Fucking numbnuts," Chad said, pushing himself from the open railing running the length of the bow. Even the dogs were made to look like fools as they were jerked out of their restful postures, regaining then losing their feet, their heavy rough pads sliding atop the wet deck.

"Are we here?" Nick asked.

"Couldn't be anywhere else," Erik said.

"Russell," Chad said. "You stay here and be ready to git, huh?"

Russell nodded. Chad gave Nick a point toward the shore. "There it is: Land. Go." Nick and Chad followed Erik from the bank to a narrow but thoroughly worn, smooth path through the vegetation. Erik led the way with a flashlight and Chad with his dogs followed with a light of his own. The thought crossed Nick's mind to take a dive into the brush, just run and extricate himself, fucking bail, make for the river and get lost in its blackness. But he didn't do it. Best case he'd be lost in blackness until morning, then still fifty miles from anywhere with no ride but his boots.

The path led to a small shack, no larger than the box belonging to the cow men at the ferry crossing. Inside the shack the dimmest flicker of flame shone from an oil-filled lantern, lashing out like a tongue to wet the splintery walls with light. The men and dogs went into the shack and waited for them. Inside was Hobo, tied up, no gag. Nick figured keeping him quiet wasn't necessary since he was miles away from anyone who could have heard him scream. Nick also realized that he was in the same place.

"You know this guy, yeah?" Chad said.

Nick nodded.

"What the hell's going on, Nick?" Hobo said,

teeth chattering. He was unscathed, but rightly concerned. He shivered in his cold, pissed pants.

"He don't know anything," Chad said. He gave a short whistle and the dogs standing at his feet pricked up their ears.

"Nick! What do they want?" Hobo said.

Nick shook his head and began to repeat what Chad had told him. "Fuckface," Chad said, "he doesn't know!"

Nick wondered what he'd do if a weapon materialized. The answer, of course, was nothing. What could he do? Get shot or torn up.

"I'll tell you why you're here. Number one, you lied to me. You said a pound last night and that's what was expected. But that's only part of it. Truth is, you can't be trusted. Didn't even let your partner in on the deal. That's what you said, right Nick? 'I didn't know you were working with Hobo.'"

Nick opened his mouth but no words came. He felt the same hot shame he'd felt for Kimmy when he thought she was powerless against the blonde at Nate's. And for a moment Nick envied Hobo's position in the chair. But that was short lived.

"Git 'em," was all Chad said and then the dogs were on Hobo and it was messy as you'd expect. Helpless was the only way to feel, and horrified, watching the pieces of Hobo as they practically fell away from his frame and into the hot gullets of the beasts.

"What the fuck?" Nick said. "Stop them! Please!"

Chad continued walking. "What the fuck what? Too late for stops."

"The shit was between me and him and he gets fucking eaten over it?! That's fucking overkill, don't you think?"

Chad turned, met Nick's hot eyes with a look of open-wound hurt. "Maybe," he said, "but the job gets done my way just fine." He began walking to the boat again but stopped, as if he was thinking about which way to go. He turned back to Nick. "Old life is old life, doesn't matter. You're with us now." He held his gaze for a long time, waiting, ready for Nick to reject the gift. "And there's no overkill," he added. "Dead is dead."

Nick followed with the dogs close behind, licking their chops. Nick felt for the Makarov though he knew it wasn't there. Perhaps another him in another universe was about to take the shot, but all he could do was stare at the back of Chad's head and imagine. Chad stopped and turned and met Nick's eye but shifted his gaze to the dogs. They stopped at Chad's heels, tails wagging. Then one of them coughed up a finger. It quickly lapped it up again and followed Chad onto the boat. Russell piloted the vessel, turning it portside and taking them back the way they came, against the current.

"Got a job for you tomorrow, Nick." Chad looked at his watch. "Today I mean."

Nick couldn't speak. Couldn't ask what. All he saw was Hobo, pieces of him.

"You like helping Kimmy so much," Chad said, turning to Nick and winking, "you can do it full time."

Six

THE SUN WAS nearly up before Chad dropped him in front of his house without a word, with four hundred dollars in worn twenties. It wasn't much higher in the sky when pounding on his front door woke Nick with a start.

He opened the door to find Kimmy on the porch. Her bruised, swollen face and crooked grin reminded him of a jack-o-lantern two weeks after Halloween. She was out of the sling so he supposed she was on the mend.

He stared at her, making her speak first.

"I'm sorry," she said. "They made me. I appreciate the ride though. For getting me out of there. You're sweet."

Nick shook his head, incredulous. The girl was convincing on the video. Nick would have taken her at her word, upset as she was, except he knew the truth. And now she was here to sweet talk him into God knew what.

"Think it's a good idea to be here?" Nick asked. "Charges and all?"

"They ain't gonna go anywhere with that. As long

as," she stopped.

"As long as I behave?"

"Long as." She grinned.

They stood in silence a moment. She fumbled with a cigarette and he helped her. He searched for her eyes but they were quick to dart away and obscured by the swelling. She smoked, smiled, didn't speak.

"So what do you want?" Nick said.

"I want you to take me to my mom's so I can see my kid."

"Sounds like boyfriend work."

"He don't have time for all that. Besides, his boys do errands for me all the time."

"I'm not one of his boys."

"You stole that cow with them. You're one of his boys. That's what he does, finds what he wants then finds a way to keep it close."

"That how he's keeping you so close? By letting me run you all over town?"

"Get over yourself, boy. Drive me." She handed off the key to the Volkswagen, turned around slowly, and got in the passenger seat. They looked at one another through the windshield for a moment before she threw up a hand and began honking the horn.

Nick relented. "I've got to get dressed," he said. "Cut it out with the fucking horn."

Nick closed the door and looked out the peep

while he evaluated the freshness of his shit sandwich. Best case he was initiated into the company of some dangerous folks, worst case he was in for some real kind of hurt. And the rub was that the two scenarios weren't mutually exclusive.

Nick showered quickly and threw on a clean t-shirt and jeans. From the top drawer, under his socks, he pulled up the false bottom and grabbed his piece, a Makarov 9x18 he hadn't shot in years, and for a moment it was like he was looking through Hobo's eyes—soulmates in nerves, headfirst into a situation they wish they could've stayed the hell away from.

Nick checked the clip and put one in the chamber. The gun was part of a lot he'd bought from a frat kid turned tweeker back in college. Nick and the kid, Victor Anastas, were both taking target shooting for a PE credit and the kid's family had an extensive stockpile of Soviet weapons. They figured the class would be a good place to get some much needed cash. Victor said his grandfather was some eastern bloc munitions guy and he'd spent most of the 1980s sending them to a relative in Canada. Nick walked away from the deal with three Makarovs (two shit, one beauty) and more Soviet 9x18s than he could ever shoot. The deal had cost him his textbook money for the semester, but it was too good to pass up. It was two years later, after Nick had been kicked out of school, that he heard the guy, the frat boy tweeker Victor, ate one of those Russian shells for breakfast.

Nick tucked the gun into the back of his pants and left the house. Kimmy was waiting, reading a celebrity magazine and sipping from a McDonald's cup. Nick got in the driver side, smelled whiskey. He sat and watched as Kimmy added a healthy shot from a pint of Kessler's, recapped the cup and sucked from the straw. Her eyes shifted to Nick and she pounded on the dashboard, wincing as she again forgot the headgear and tried to turn her head.

"Let's go."

"Where we going?" Nick asked.

"Just get on the eastbound and I'll get us there."

Nick backed out of the drive. Kimmy continued slurping from the cup. He drove.

"Your wife died," Kimmy said.

It was the way a child would broach the subject. He looked at her and chuckled. She couldn't look at him, only straight ahead.

"Yes," Nick said.

"A kid too?"

"Stillborn, but yeah. Killed herself and the baby."

"How come?" Kimmy asked.

The questions didn't sting the way Nick thought they should. Nor did they rile him with their absence of compassion and tact. It was seven years ago and he had long given up trying to climb back up the rock he'd been thrown from; he'd acquiesced to reality and continued from below, on a different path for a different man.

"She wasn't happy," Nick said. "With me. With anything."

"I lost my girl. Taken away, I mean. You know that?"

"I didn't," Nick said, uninterested. "I don't really know you. Just from the bar."

Kimmy took a long pull from her straw, slurping the remains. "My girl, my Janie, isn't Chad's. If she was she wouldn't be living with my mama. Should be enough she's mine, but Chad doesn't care. It isn't his, so why bother? He took Tommy away too, that's her daddy, had him put away. Put him away and took the only thing I had left of him from me."

"They don't take a kid away for nothing," Nick said, borrowing her lack of tact. "Why'd they take her?"

Kimmy remained quiet, pointed to a McDonald's. "I need a refill." She went back to her magazine, apparently tired of conversation.

***

Kimmy's mother lived twenty-five dirt-road miles east

of Horton and most of that was driven in silence. Kimmy didn't speak again except to tell him when to get off the highway and which way to turn.

"Why do you need me to do this?" Nick finally asked.

"You think I'm in any condition to drive?" Kimmy laughed.

"You in any condition to see your kid?" Nick asked. It wasn't his business and he didn't truly care, but that part of him that was poised to turn father when Grete was expecting hadn't completely eroded. Same with the husband part. A little hiccup of brain chemistry lit up the abandoned paths; the same part that had gotten him into this mess, biology trumping common sense.

Kimmy slurped the last of her drink and raised the empty pint to her eyes. She threw both the cup and the glass pint out the window of the car. The bottle hit the tall roadside weeds with a gasp. Nick kept his eyes on the empty road. More silence.

"No. I suppose not," Kimmy said after a time, still on the question of her condition. "But it's expected." She rested her haloed head against the window with a metallic clink. The sound continued as the little Volkswagen bounced on the pocked country road. She remained still and Nick thought she'd fallen asleep, until finally she pointed. "It's up here on the left. Slow down or you'll miss it."

Nick saw no driveway until he was on it, no more than a narrow break in the tall green corn that dominated the area. He pulled into the rutted dirt drive and the car was immediately swallowed up whole by thick stalks. The long, straight gravel drive was dark, shaded with little slashes of sunlight that ripped through narrow breaks and turned the corn stalks into shadowy fingers that bad-touched everything that dared come close.

"I hate coming back here," Kimmy said.

The gravel gave way to dirt, then that gave way to a narrow strip of brown grass in front of the house. A clean pink manufactured home, single level with black metal stairs up to the small porch and door. A strip of lawn wrapped around the property, giving about fifteen feet of relief from the surrounding corn. Nick looked up to the house and saw a little white face pressed against the window. An older white face appeared above. The fresh eyes paused on him, but they quickly found Kimmy. The woman rolled her eyes and headed toward the door.

"Uh uh! No way, girl!" the woman hollered as she opened the door. "You ain't supposed to be within two hundred feet. I'll call the law, don't you think I won't."

"Can I just see her, mama?" Kimmy's voice

croaked, lost the apathy she'd projected in the car. "I'll stay away. I just want to see my Janie!"

Kimmy's mother looked at her daughter as if all the love she'd had was beaten out of her. She shook her head and looked to Nick.

"You do that to her?" Kimmy's mother said.

Nick shook his head. "I'm just a ride."

"Hmmph. And what kind of ride is that?" Kimmy's mother looked from Nick to Kimmy to the little girl watching the scene through a birdshit-spattered window. The little thing behind the glass was blonde and had the look of her mother, her grandmother, her wide doe eyes bright, yet uncertain as they found Nick. The elder Flynn woman was quite pretty, and tired, a gray extrapolation of Kimmy's timeline.

Kimmy's mother gave up, threw her hands in the air. "Well now she's seen you. You can come in for five minutes, that's it." She looked at Nick. "He ain't."

Nick stepped off the porch, glad to be excluded. He leaned on the hood of Kimmy's car and listened to the corn whisper and rub in the breeze. Crows, a lot of goddamn crows, hopped from the corn and into the yard. Some launched up and settled on the roof of the trailer home while others flew off, and the remainder hopped back into the corn, one after the other.

Kimmy stepped from the house quicker than Nick had expected, even as bad as her mother wanted her out. The elder Flynn followed her out, but held fast at the doorway.

"You don't come back!" she screamed.

Nick watched the young girl, still at the window, seemingly unmoved.

"This is it! Don't you come back!"

Kimmy moved past Nick and grabbed a rusted shovel that leaned against the house. "C'mon," she said, stepping into the thick of the corn, right behind a pair of crows.

Nick fought through the stalks, searched for Kimmy's form in the shadow, found her briefly in the small patches of light. She cut left and he followed.

"Where the hell we going?" Nick said.

Kimmy slowed and turned as much as her bones would allow. She handed over the shovel. "Take this," she said. She cut into a new row, walked the same direction they'd started in.

"Ever see a scarecrow?" she said.

Nick shook his head, confused, sweating, irritated. "No," he said. "That where we're going? To see a scarecrow?"

She laughed. "No. I asked if you've *seen* one."

"Not a for real one, like in the middle of a field like this, no."

"They don't work. They don't keep nothing away. If anything, they bring the crows. They figure it out real quick that there must be something really valuable, really worth protecting if someone goes to the trouble of stuffing a man full of straw and posting him up in a field. Crows are smart birds."

"So I'm told," Nick said. "Where the hell are you taking me, Kimmy? I know you think I'm your personal assistant or something now, errand boy or whatever, but I got shit to do. My own shit."

"No, you don't," she said, then cut left again. Nick could only follow. Before he could protest, they stepped out of the cornfield and were on a steep slope with a stream below. The sun shone bright and green through the leaves.

"We got to cross it," Kimmy said. "Help me."

Nick sidestepped down the slope first, stabbed the shovel into the bank for balance. He took Kimmy's waiting hand and helped her step into the creek bed. The clear water ran shallow around a deposit of smooth black stones. She pulled her hand from his and stepped onto the stones and hopped to the other side. She turned herself around.

"It's safe," she said. "I put them there years ago. Just step straight down, they're slippery."

The rocks *were* slippery, like black ice and Nick fought against their smooth pull to no avail. A few slippery kicks and waving arms were all the fight he had in him as he upended and landed hard in the shallow water.

"Goddamnit!"

Kimmy couldn't stop laughing as Nick pulled himself to his feet, nearly losing his footing again. With angry haste and an aching tailbone, Nick stepped out of the water, dripping as he took her hand roughly and helped her up the steep bank. Kimmy took the lead again and Nick followed her into a wood that grew thick as the corn on the other side. He wanted to ask again where they were going but before he could speak Kimmy stopped and he found himself in a large clearing. A nearly perfect thirty-by-thirty-foot square, no life inside.

"Some drunk aliens do this?" Nick said.

Kimmy almost smiled. "I sterilized it," she said. "Didn't want anything growing here. Ever."

She crossed to the far side of the square and examined the tree line, looking for something: a large knot in the ancient black oak. She turned her back to it, butted herself right up against it and counted off paces. Her stride was abbreviated, like she was following the tracks of another, smaller, younger person. She stopped at thirteen paces before beginning again at 'one' and counting out another unlucky number of paces. Nick watched as Kimmy took a deep breath and bowed her head as if saying a silent prayer, or possibly a curse, for the ground she stood on.

"This is it," she said. She turned to Nick. "This is it," she said again. "Bring that shovel and start digging right here." She tapped her sandaled foot on the ground. Her feet were dirty and her toes bled from tiny briar scratches.

Nick dug and she watched. The ground was soft and it made for easy work, but the easy added up and soon Nick was wet with sweat, standing in his hole with a growing pile of "easy" behind him. Waist deep in the hole he wiped his brow and looked at Kimmy and wondered if he was actually digging something up or preparing a grave.

The shovel hit something hard. He widened the hole and looked at Kimmy. The noise had drawn her attention from the trees.

"That's it. That's the door. Clear it."

Nick's digging took on an artist's purpose as he used the shovel to pull away what it was he didn't want. When Nick finished he was standing in a hole, four feet across both ways and three feet deep. Exposed on one side was a piece of particle board with a rope knotted through near the top edge. Kimmy came closer.

"Now pull that thing out. Please."

Nick climbed out of the hole and took the rope in his hands. He pulled hard but the wood came loose easily, straight up and smooth as butter. Nick's inertia nearly put him on his ass again. He ignored Kimmy's amusement, tossed the wood aside with a grunt, and looked into the square doorway carved into the earth. The smell of death was a punch in the nose.

"Now what?" Nick said, bringing his elbow pit to his nose. "Ah, Christ!" It was the blonde girl from Nate's, face a mess of dried blood and swell, very dead.

"Never mind her. Now you go in there and pull out what you find."

Nick dropped the shovel and its head sang out against a rock. He stepped back into the hole. He had no flashlight but the sunlight was bright enough that his eyes adjusted quickly. Through the doorway was a chamber, twice the size of the hole he'd dug. The chamber's walls were made of the same wood as the door. The ceiling, too, was held up and braced with cedar four by fours. About halfway back he saw mason jars stacked neatly and tightly from wall to wall, floor to ceiling. He looked closer and saw the jars were full of coins, all quarters by the look of it.

"Is it still there?" Kimmy called from above ground.

"Yeah," Nick said, gagging on the smell.

He popped his head out of the chamber, pulled himself out and put two of the jars at the edge of the hole. The quarters inside were clean and shining. "There's got to be thousands in quarters here."

"Four thousand, three hundred seventy-two dollars and fifty cents," Kimmy said.

Nick laughed despite himself, despite the dirt and sweat. "Hell of a piggy bank. Where'd you get this?"

"Get the rest of them and I'll show you. You'll never believe me if I tell you."

Nick looked at her. She was smiling at the jars the same way she'd smiled at her girl through the window. Nick went back in for more of the jars, his curiosity aroused.

There were sixty-two jars in all, and Nick carried every one of them, four at a time, back to the car. By the time he finished the day had slipped away to dusk. Kimmy waited at the car.

"So you going to tell me what's up with these? You rob an arcade?"

"Didn't rob anyone, not really. Nobody who'd miss it anyway. Come with me."

Nick followed her behind the house to a small wooden shed butted up to the cornfield. Kimmy opened the door and pointed to a large wooden box, again constructed of the same particle board that formed the vault. "Pull that thing out for me." The box was on small castor wheels that dug into the grass as Nick dragged it from the shed.

Kimmy opened a jar and took a handful of quarters. She looked at Nick and flashed a smile. "Watch," she whispered, and threw the quarters into the air. For a moment they were lost against the bright flare of the sun, then just as quickly reappeared in the grass before vanishing again, this time beneath the beating of black wings.

Nick watched as more and more crows descended on the yard, each coin found and retrieved by a different bird. Nick sat dumbstruck as the birds, one by one, perched atop the wooden box and deposited the coins into a barely visible slot. On the side facing Nick and Kimmy, near the bottom, a small amount of yellow meal corn flowed from a round hole, catching in a small plastic cup fixed to the box with duct tape.

Nick watched, an incredulous grin on his face. "It's a fucking crow vending machine."

Kimmy laughed. "Yes. A fucking crow vending machine."

The pair was silent as crow after crow deposited quarter after quarter, and the corn did flow. When it stopped, the crows knew it and looked at Kimmy, hundreds of them, lining the gutters of the pink house, perched wing to wing. Others covered the box, the yard, and more and more emerged from the field.

Kimmy walked to the shed and returned with a bucket. She dipped her hand and threw handfuls of corn over the yard. The birds descended. The sound of wings flapped against the stale air. Nick felt the breeze of their collective effort and he laughed to himself as the cooler air hit his face. He looked at Kimmy, but she only had eyes for the crows, until she found her daughter in the small window of a bathroom at the back of the house. Kimmy dropped the bucket, spilling corn and leaving it to be swarmed by the birds. The young girl smiled and slid the dirty glass in its track, leaned out to touch her mother. Kimmy stepped up on a waiting apple crate and touched the girl's face.

"Tell me again about the scarecrow man, Mama."

"It happened in the summer," Kimmy said. "When the corn was tall, that's when the scarecrow man would come home. And when he came home he stole things from the girl. He said it was only to borrow, that he'd return it, and it would be better because only by losing something could people, especially little girls, really feel the gifts they got. Like how when the scarecrow man was away, he said he missed her so much, and how he thought of her all the time, with every crow he swatted from the air—with every neck he broke with a quick twist of his strong hands. His rough hands. He'd kiss her neck, year after year, when it was time to cut down the corn. 'I'm back,' he'd say. 'What do you have for me?' And each time she had less and less. Because he'd lied to the girl and he never returned the things he borrowed. And she had nothing to compare against her loss and it was that way for a long, long time. So she had to find something that was hers, something that no one knew about. So she buried it and then, no matter what he took, even when he took away everything, she could think on what she had, her secret, and then she could smile the way he liked her to. Say the sweet words he gave her to say."

"He's gone, Mama?"

Kimmy smiled. "Don't worry." She stroked her daughter's nearly white hair. "Do you want to hear the rest?"

The girl nodded.

Nick's gaze returned to the crows as they ate. When the birds had finished what Kimmy threw, they looked at Nick and hopped closer. Nick threw more corn and again the air beat against his ears.

Kimmy looked into her daughter's eyes. "The rest is," she hesitated, looked back at Nick. "The rest is that everything worked out for the girl and everyone she loved became very, very happy." And she touched her daughter again.

"Don't cry, Mama," the child said.

"Okay," Kimmy said, wiping her eyes. "I won't."

"Can I come with you, Mama?"

"Not yet, baby. Soon. Soon."

Kimmy reached out again but the girl disappeared and Kimmy's own mother stood in her place. Kimmy's hands went to her sides.

"Don't come back again," the woman said, then shut the window and drew the shade. Kimmy hopped from her perch and looked at Nick and wiped her eyes.

"Family, huh?" she said.

***

The rural road was dark and the inside of the VW glowed low from the dashboard light. The road was cracked and each jostling bump of the concrete made the coins ring out from the jars.

"So what's with the fucking coins," Nick said.

"Been saving up."

"How long?"

"Started at twelve years old. Stopped when I left the house. Seventeen."

"All from the birds?"

She looked at him. He kept his eyes on the road. "All from them."

"Hadn't thought about it," Nick said. "More of a

plants guy."

"They make tools. You know that? Give them a wire and they can shape it into a hook. Use it to unlock doors, grab things out of reach."

"No. I didn't know that. How'd you learn about it? Thought you were an art student."

"Mom shacked up with a bird guy for a while. He's the one built the machine. Showed me how easy training crows was. You want to know what the coins are for?"

"I do," Nick started. "But I feel like I'd be better off not knowing."

"I've got somebody who's going to kill that son of a bitch for me."

"'Cause he beat you up?"

"You call this beat up? That son of a bitch tried to kill me. My eye socket is busted under here. My face isn't going to look the same." She trailed off. "Not like it did."

"But that ain't all the reason," she said. "I know how to get into his safe. I get the money out of the safe and I get myself set up right, show the state I can take care of my girl. Get her out of that shithole I was raised in."

Nick looked at her, tried to gauge her earnestness, but she stared straight ahead. "You're going to get yourself killed. The poor sap you pay off is going to get killed. You've seen his dogs, right? Anybody tries anything they're getting torn up. They look like they'd take a couple of slugs and like it."

Kimmy looked out the window, stared at the invisible scenery. She sighed, seemingly dejected. She lit a fresh cigarette from the butt of the old and took a long drag. "I've got the dogs figured." She took another drag. "Just about."

And just like that she lost the will to chat. After a while, Nick said, "Why are you telling me this? Aren't you afraid I'll tell him? Part of the crew and all?"

"No. You don't seem like the talking type. And you might be *in* the crew, but you aren't crew. You fell in because it was either adopt you or kill you. And whatever the reason, you got adopted. Like me. Brought me in and here I am, like it or not."

"It's because I know cows," Nick said. "And because I've got nothing better to do than drive you, I guess."

She looked at him with a confused squint, then her eyes cleared as the pieces of some inner puzzle fit into place for her. She sat back and fell into shadow, out of the dashboard light's reach.

"Shame about the church, huh?" Kimmy said.

"Church? Oh, yeah. The burned one, sure."

"You know it was the oldest building in Jessup?"

"You're just full of fun facts, aren't you?"

That quieted her again. They drove and the coins jingled and after a time the meager cityscape of Horton became visible in the distance. The brightest, highest structures were fast food signs put up to attract highway traffic. And behind the restaurants and the competing gas stations you could locate Sokja's Chevy lot by its swaying spotlight that burned and cut through the dark every night.

***

Nick stepped out of the car, the air, calm but rife with menace. He looked over his shoulder, down the quiet street, then turned and looked the other way. Nothing visible, but he felt eyes on him nonetheless.

Kimmy stepped around the front of the car toward him. He backed up and let her pass in front and take her place behind the wheel. She turned her head gingerly.

"Thanks for the help," she said.

Nick shrugged and looked away.

"I need you to take me to school tomorrow. And stop at the vet for me? You can take me to lunch."

"If Chad doesn't want me someplace else."

"He don't," she said, starting the car. Then she was gone.

Seven

SHE'D BEEN POUNDING on the door for fifteen minutes before Nick woke from a dream of hammering old wooden coffins together.

He looked out the peep. She was crying, her eyeliner running from her bruised eyes and streaking down both cheeks.

"Christ," Nick said to himself.

"Let me in," she said as he unchained the door. He opened it and stepped back a few feet.

"I got robbed. That asshole took the money and said to go ahead and sic the dogs on him so he could tell Chad what the money was for."

"You didn't consider that?"

"No. I did but then I decided to risk it." She looked at him and Nick realized that he was the justification for her risk, and he wondered if he was anything more than another dog.

"You expect me to do something about it?"

She laughed and the tears were dry. "He tell you not to fuck his goat yet?"

Nick didn't answer, just kept looking into her one open eye.

"Baaah!" She let the sound become a laugh. "I'll tell him you were good at least; that after you forced yourself on me it was," she breathed out, "kind of nice. Romantic even." She stepped closer and Nick stepped back and she was laughing again.

"Too much?" she asked. "C'mon."

He looked at her and wondered about her seriousness, if she never was or always was.

"Tell me what the coins were for."

"I told you what they were for."

"You were collecting long before you knew Chad."

She hesitated, took great care with what she chose to say next. "It was for something else I ended up not needing done. I heard what he did to your friend."

That she knew as much as she did threw him and all he could say was, "Wasn't really a friend."

"But friendly," she said. "You live alone here since your wife died, right? Lonely maybe. Guilty? Dead guy was the closest thing to a friend anyway. Chad does that. He makes himself everything you need by taking away everything else. I told you."

Nick sighed and had to smile. The girl was as tenacious as one of the mutts. "You're going to end up getting me killed," he said. "Who the hell am I dealing with for you?"

"No one important," she said.

***

No one important turned out to be the Horton chief of police. And though Chief probably liked the sound of his own name, the way it hit his ears and timbered on the eardrum, like an axe chop followed by hard broom across concrete, it raised the hairs on Nick's neck every time he heard it.

"Unfucking believable," Nick said, as they sat in the VW. The top was down and the smell on the summer breeze was honeysuckle, but it did nothing for the unnerving dread that had been rising since she told her story. She told him Chief had shot and killed three men in a city with exactly zero intentional shooting injuries, police or otherwise, in one-hundred fifty years. She said he was known to provide many services beyond the routine work of police chief. He was a dangerous man and now here Nick was playing lookout while Kimmy searched for her coins.

"You don't even know if they're still there."

"They're there."

They watched Chief step out; huge, he lumbered down the steps of the station and got into the already running, AC-cooled cruiser. His destination was unknown but he seemed in a hurry, lights flashing but no siren. The cruiser bottomed out hard as the steep drive met the road. The V-8 rumbled away and Kimmy got out of the VW.

"I'll look for the coins. When I signal, you back up to the front steps."

"We're going to die, Kimmy. Both of us."

"Not today," she said and slammed the door. She walked across the street and went in the front entrance of the unmanned station, and Nick realized Kimmy had lifted a ring of keys from the station after Chief had burned her over the coins, the driving to Nick's and turning on the faucets.

Nick tuned the radio but quickly shut it down to focus on the station. Two girls on bicycles pedaled past, in and out of Nick's gaze. He dreaded a run-in with Chief, another dangerous man inserted into this bizarre fiasco. Nick managed to stay off the man's radar for all his dealing years, but now he was front and center with Kimmy's story. Would they go through with it? Would she hold fast to the lie she told the camera? Best he could hope was that she was successful in her plan. Chad dead and gone, things would go back to normal. Maybe Grete wouldn't haunt his garage with the smell of exhaust anymore. Perhaps she would be alive again and not stuck in bed with a sadness he resented as he shuffled to work every morning at four, then found her in the same place when he returned in the afternoon. At first Nick had tried attentive care, but he couldn't understand why she couldn't snap out of it. After two months Nick began to waver between feelings of resentment and the general frustration he'd had since he first mentioned a doctor.

"I don't want a doctor." The words came out of her like hot spit.

"You don't want to get better?"

"I don't want to get better."

She rolled over and hid from him, as she did now, and he stormed around the bed to face her.

"No!" he said. "What is this?"

"It's my life," she said. She was rubbing her swollen belly beneath the blanket. Her face was black, gaze empty, the brick of the old walls reflected in her wet eyes. She turned her eyes from the wall. "This is me," and she punctuated her reply by rolling away from him.

It was then he began spending his evenings at Nate's, drinking himself tired then coming home to her, sometimes watching her sleep before passing out in whatever corner of the house he'd end up. But first he watched, and her hands were never away from the near full-term baby inside her. And he wondered how long he should wait, for the baby's sake, to have her committed. But he never got to make that call. She'd surprised him. Showed up at the golf course for a reason he never learned. He was up at the clubhouse talking to that fucker Kurt DeVries about the rumors going round. Kurt spoke in hushed tones and Nick tried to listen. He knew it was serious but she caught his eye, giant sunglasses hiding her face. She was in their car and wearing the pink bathrobe he hadn't seen her out of in a trimester.

"These are serious allegations, Nick," Kurt was saying. Nick looked at him.

"Allegations," Nick said. "That's all." Then his attention was on the lot. The Shelby began to move, behind a stand of pines that blocked the lot from the practice range, and she was gone.

"If I go to the board with this."

Nick shrugged it off, confident that a club member's privacy would trump any complaint of illicit activity. He sold to some folks in the community who, though it was just a little marijuana, still had to maintain certain appearances. But Nick soon learned how serious Kurt was. He did go to the board, and Nick was pulled in that very day. And there on the table, between Nick and the five white-haired men, was a plastic bag containing a quarter ounce of pot. Nick knew it was his, but could they prove it? Didn't matter. They didn't have to. He could leave quietly with a small severance. "Baby on the way and all." Or he could fight them, and yes, he might damage a reputation or two, but he was certain to find himself in a world of legal hurt. He didn't want that, did he? Again, "baby on the way and all."

Nick hated that he still had to think about this shit. So much later but here he was, still thinking as he waited, his mind a slave to the past. Nick felt the breeze and listened to the rough rustle of leaves shivering in his ears and making him nervous. He thought she'd be in and out but she was taking her time and Nick was nervous. He'd spent as much time with Chief as he cared to. But the alternative was Chad, and even though Nick knew that everyone involved was likely to end up in a worse spot if Kimmy were good to her word, Nick couldn't argue that the man needed to go. After seeing what he'd done to Kimmy, not that he'd hurt her, but to the extent Chad was able to do so and laugh about it—or show nothing but a glow of privileged confidence, mistaking the ability to hurt with the right to do so.

If Nick already knew he'd be in a worse spot, he knew it completely when Chief's cruiser returned.

Nick stepped out of the car and Chief turned to the running footsteps just as he began climbing the station steps. Nick stopped two steps below, craned his neck to look up at the towering man. He said the first thing he could think of.

"I want the tape."

The big man grinned. "I'm sure you do. You're in quite a spot now, aren't you?"

Nick looked past Chief's shoulder into the front glass for a glimpse of Kimmy. He looked into Chief's brown aviators. "What's it going to take?" he said.

"More than you got I'm sure. Now if you don't mind," Chief said. "Fucking go. Be a good little shit and get the fuck out of my face!" Chief stepped quickly toward him and Nick took a defensive step back down the stairs, stumbling. Chief laughed and left him be. Nick watched him climb the stairs—with Kimmy still inside.

Nick stood helpless as Chief entered the building. He didn't know whether to go inside or run. He did neither as Kimmy was then at the glass, waving him up to the door.

Inside, past the small lobby, Chief lay on the floor, moaning and bleeding from the head. Kimmy stepped over him and hovered, the extendable baton at her side.

"Get the cuffs on him," Kimmy said.

"What the fuck did you do? Where are your coins?"

"Not here. I didn't have time to ask him. Now get those cuffs on him 'fore he wakes up!"

Chief began to stir and Kimmy gave him another hard crack on the skull. Nick hesitated as he thought about his spot. Realized he was fucked upon fucked upon fucked. He dropped to his knees and fished Chief's cuffs from him. Nick closed them tight around the thick apish wrists behind the man's back. Then he removed the man's belt and all the accompanying gadgets.

Chief stirred again and this time Kimmy helped get him to his feet. He began to struggle as soon as he got up. A beast, he threw his shoulder hard into Nick and sent him sprawling. Nick watched the man turn on Kimmy, sending her to the floor with a hard kick in the stomach as she raised the baton, then going to work on her hands with the sole of his heavy boots as she tried to retrieve the metal club skittering across the dirty black linoleum.

Nick launched himself hard and drove his shoulder into Chief's back. The big man squealed and there was an unnatural pop. For a moment no one moved, Chief on one knee, Nick ready to strike, Kimmy crawling on stomped hands for the baton. Then Chief took a hard step up. Another pop and a gentler squeal as he turned, face a fire of red and sweat and snot. It was only a moment but that was all he needed as the handcuffs dropped to the floor. Chief tossed the key at Nick who let it bounce off his chest.

"Always keep a cuff key in your ass crack," Chief said. "First rule of surviving a couple of dumb shits like you." The giant felt for his back and winced, dropping again to his knee, but only long enough to pull a .25 caliber from his boot. He drew on the pair and as Nick's guts nearly fell through his asshole, he lost any interest in the sincerity of Chief's statement about where he hid spare keys.

"I should kill the both of you right now." He stopped and looked at Nick. Something of a smile stretched across his face. "I figured you'd bring this one around," he said to Kimmy. "Didn't figure you to ring my bell though. Capable girl."

The trio stood silent, still huffing and tired, sweating from the burst of exertion, cooling in the frigid air conditioning of the Horton Police Station.

Chief stepped forward and neither Nick nor Kimmy dared move. Chief kept the piece on Nick and grabbed his baton from the floor. He raised it without looking and gave Kimmy a hard tap on the headgear that made it sing, before using the prod to usher her out of his blind. Chief stood her with Nick, who took a quick look over his shoulder for the exit. Chief glared at them the way a father looks down on the bad children he's caught red-handed in some deed so ridiculous only a child could have thought of it.

"I got the money. It's mine and you're not getting it back," he said to Kimmy. Then he looked again to Nick. "But the job will get done. Don't worry. I'm going to subcontract it. Payment is your life, Nick. Free and clear. You keep growing. I'll take your harvest. Name your price. Fair price. You decide to hang up the spurs, knock yourself unconscious, I won't force you."

"Why don't you just do it?" Nick said.

Chief laughed. "I'm not strong the way Chad is. I mean I could whip him in a fair one, no dogs. But even that ain't worth a sack of sand. See, what I've got is Power. And Power means I don't *need* to do it."

Chief turned to Kimmy. "I'm sorry about the boot and I'm sorry I led you to believe I'm less than fair. I make a deal and I stick by it." He looked at Nick again. "And that's what I expect out of anyone I deal with. I see how far you're willing to go. You're going to go a little further and you're going to take care of this. You got every reason in the world far as I'm concerned." Chief grinned and Nick couldn't do a thing but take the big man's outstretched hand. Chief pumped it vigorously and held that all-knowing grin. Nick returned the smile and wondered how a single pawn stood a chance in three simultaneous games.

Eight

LIFE SEEMED REASONABLY normal for Nick during the next few days, which was a surprise seeing as he had such abnormal business to take care of. Like the cosmos were playing a joke on him, making the job ahead of him loom darker and more oppressive by comparison.

He hadn't heard from Chad, Kimmy, or Chief in a couple days, but the trio were still on his mind, waking him in the night from dreams of dogs and blood. He thought about Hobo and looked at the clock. Time for a drink.

When he stepped into Nate's the twisted man looked at him with a grin before scuttling to the tap to get him a beer. Nick took his stool at the end of the bar. The Gebbins Hardware bag still sat on the back of the bar on top of the mini-fridge.

"Getting right on that lock, huh?" Nick said after a long pull on his beer. Nate just smiled and shrugged.

"I'll get to it."

Nate turned on the TV and left Nick while he tended to business at the other end of the bar, filling small plastic containers with supplies for the night:

lemon and lime slices, cherries, olives, and baby onions. Nate was never much of a talker, but he was quiet tonight even for him.

"Cat got your tongue? Or maybe a dog or two?"

At first Nick thought he wasn't going to answer. But finally Nate looked up from the fruit and vegetables that had demanded his attention.

"I'm sorry for you, Nick. I wish I could have warned you."

Nick wondered how much Nate knew about his situation, and how much of it was simply experience as one of Chad's lackeys. He'd surely seen a lot over the years.

"I'll be okay."

"You think?" Nate said.

Nick watched the twisted man as he continued to wipe down the clean bar. He wanted to be angry, wanted someone to blame, but he knew there was no one at fault but himself. Everything that had happened since the night he'd driven Kimmy home was nothing but part of a natural progression of events that should have been seen—would have been seen by someone with a little more sense. But he felt for Nate, knew that Chad's patronage was the thing that kept Nate's going. And Nick couldn't expect old Nate to help him, if Nick himself couldn't refuse to submit, how could he expect it from old, twisted

Nate? But still, he sensed an advantage, and perhaps it was the company he was keeping. He decided to use it.

"Play a song for me, huh?" Nick said. The man looked at him, his lips twitching from side to side, like the wagging tail of a dog that can't quite make a decision.

"Okay," he said.

The piano in the corner was as clean as the bar though he knew Nate rarely played it anymore. But he kept it dusted and shined, and Nick had seen him tune it on several occasions. Nate took a seat on the bench and lifted the key cover. Nick watched from behind as the skinny little man's fingers came to life and descended on the faux ivory. Then his digits danced like a man who hadn't been afflicted by an archaic virus. He leaned heavily to the right, and to compensate for the reach, Nate had to slide his body left to reach the lower notes. But it was just as natural as the ease of his fingers on the keys.

Nate had known the song to play. And Nick thought of his wife, the nights he'd spent with her alone in the bar, making small talk while they listened to the music—alcohol fueling their honesty and their joy. Until it didn't.

A case of the "baby blues" she had called it, this pregnancy thing. And the descent was absolute, but gradually so, though he wanted to be her rock and did what he could. There was the golf course to care for, especially since she had quit teaching and his was the only income. It was stressful. And when he found the group of club members who relished a good crop of marijuana, things became easier, though not at home. So Nick kept up appearances at Nate's, alone, drinking into the night, and arriving home to find her where he'd left her in the blue light of the television. He always tried not to wake her as he used the restroom, draining an evening's worth of beer. But always when he came back to the living room he knew he'd been too loud. Grete would have already retreated into the darkness of their bedroom, unreachable.

Still listening to Nate play, Nick fished his vibrating phone from his pocket.

"Hello?"

The sound of crashing bowling pins and cheers drowned out the low voice.

"What?"

"Chad wants you at the bowling alley," Russell repeated.

"What's going on?"

"Business. Get down here." Another crash, then silence as the phone went dead. Nick noticed the music had stopped and Nate was pulling himself from the piano bench. He was done playing, debt paid.

"Told me he'd be calling for you," Nate said.

"What's he want?"

Nate shrugged as he closed the wooden lid over the piano keys. "I don't know. What do I look like? The guy who knows shit?"

***

Chad Toll's truck sat taking up two handicapped spots closest to the door of Horton Lanes.

"You just getting up?" Chad said as Nick entered. "Looked for you at Nate's. Wanted to make sure things were okay. Want to bowl, man?"

Nick stood silent as Chad kneeled to scratch his dogs' heads. Behind him Russell threw a hard ball down the middle of the lane, leaving a single pin.

"You need to hook it, you dumb bastard," Erik said. "Only way to hit the pocket right."

"Yeah," Nick said to Chad. "Sure. I'll bowl."

"Get you some shoes. Let's go."

"Let's fucking bowl," Nick said.

Clown shoes in his hand, Nick joined Chad and the crew and the dogs on lane forty-two. The dogs lay out of the way under a high top table, guarding Chad's boots.

Nick was a terrible bowler and Russell and Erik let

him know it. After two miserable games Nick volunteered to get another pitcher. When Nick returned, Chad was sitting at the high top and he motioned for Nick to join him. Erik and Russell had disappeared. The bowling alley was smoke free per the state ordinance, but Chad lit a cigarette and slid his pack across the table. Nick took one and lit it. Chad topped off their beers.

"You enjoying yourself?"

"Bowling's okay."

"Not that. I mean, working with us. You happy? I know it's an adjustment, but you can write your own ticket you do right by me."

Nick just nodded. "Where are Erik and Russell?"

"Told them to go have some fun for a few hours. Russell's probably looking for tail in Grand Rapids. Erik might be with him. I really don't know. Don't care." Chad took a long drag off his cigarette. "I'm not a slave driver. May seem that way, but it's just this isn't democracy. Democracy won't work. We're a boat set to be sunk at any time. Think the captain of the boat wants to listen to everyone's opinion on the iceberg floating ahead? Shit no. He turns the fucking ship. We got Chief, but I don't trust that son of a bitch. County could come poking around. Hell, I can't trust anybody's intentions." He tapped a finger on the table, thumping it adamantly as if the idea was under dispute. "Just these bastards under the table." Chad slammed the rest of his beer and poured another. "I trust you though, Nick. You're the last of the good men."

Nick laughed. "Yeah, real good. Growing pot, stealing cattle." He leaned in despite himself, feeling the pitcher loosen his lips. "Burning down churches."

"Don't put too much stock in deed," Chad said, "if the end is noble."

"And what noble end are we reaching for?"

Chad shrugged. "Don't know yet! Ha!"

Nick laughed and said, "Was Tommy's end noble?"

Chad stopped laughing. "Whose version did you get? Hers? That son of a bitch had her blind. She was a beautiful thing and she belonged to him? You know she was just thirteen when he started in on her? Grown man messing with a child. You can't call it anything but noble."

"She doesn't see it that way."

"I knew it was her. Like I said, he got her all twisted up. He was in the wrong, doesn't matter what she thinks, foundation of her mind is built on the muck he laid down."

"You sure you just didn't want her for yourself?"

Chad laughed again, took another long pull from his plastic cup. "You watch it." He smiled. "I like you.

You want to know why? Because you're your own man. And you're smarter than most of the dumb fucks around here. I'm not claiming to be a genius but compared to most folks here, shit." He took a pull from his beer. "And you're a smart guy too, Nick. Stay smart. You're the kind of mind I want working with me. I said you're good people and I mean it. You took her home, no thought of who I was. Yeah, she gave me some of the story and I pieced together the rest from those assholes who would have let Kimmy kill that girl. You got a good foundation in you, Nick. So it doesn't matter what you do, it's going to be good."

Nick was somewhere between flattered and wanting to call bullshit on Chad's whole self-serving philosophy. He did neither.

They lit more cigarettes and poured another round from the pitcher. A group of young kids came in, the Cutter brothers and a few others, chased the goofy, little, white-haired Bizbang kid out of the arcade next to the bar.

Nick watched Chad take his place behind the computer scoring table and boot up a new set of frames. "Let's go so I can whoop you again," Chad said.

Nick studied the man as he bowled his frame. Large, but not Chief large, he threw the ball with real force, putting his will into each shot as the spinning orb curved right into that sweet spot. And Nick knew he was dealing with two men, and you never knew if he was going to bite. He'd bitten Kimmy good. He could bite anyone. But when he wasn't in the biting mood, he was a charmer. Nick didn't really care for biters or charmers and he was starting to wonder when this guy would be dead, and maybe if he wasn't the one to do it after all.

They left the bowling alley around ten o'clock and Chad pointed to his truck. "C'mon Nick, we aren't done."

Chad delivered him to the edge of the Horton Square. The street held the bulk of city parking—peppered with resident housing—all with on-street parking, four full blocks, both sides in each direction. Erik and Russell were waiting, baseball bats in hand. Chad sped away and Erik gave Nick a bat.

Nick followed the pair as they chose vehicles at random before delivering a solid strike of the aluminum bats to the windshield. Erik turned to Nick with a grin. "Fucking bust one. Earn your keep."

So Nick went to work, following the instructions, not too many on a street, a small crack better than a big one. "Don't want them all calling on the insurance tomorrow."

Nick watched Russell as he tucked a D and D

Glass Man card under the driver's side wiper of each car the trio hit.

"Who's the Glass Man?" Nick asked.

"Cousin," Russell said. "Good guy. Went to Coopersburg."

"Shut up," Erik said. "Don't tell him shit about shit."

Nick stayed quiet and let loose on another window. It was cathartic. Though the dogs yelped from blocks around, they did nothing but drown out the sound of the crime. Porch lights turned on here and there but the men passed through the shadows like ghosts.

"He's all right. He's smashing windows. Hell, he stuck his arm up a cow last night so you didn't have to."

Erik stopped and turned to Russell, looked at him with the disdain reserved for brain-damaged pets. "And he got paid for that. But this, this here is twenty-five a window split two ways and now we got to split it three? Chad doesn't want us doing more than twenty windows a week so there you go, can't make it up in production. Fucking up my shit." Erik hit another window.

"You want me gone?" Nick said. "I'll go home. Keep your cut. Jesus. Got to put my house back together anyhow."

Erik conceded nothing with his cool stare, but his eyes had lost their will to fight over the point any longer. "Isn't up to me," he said.

Nick remembered a guy from school, nice kid, choking out other kids for fun between classes. He dropped them in the hall to be stepped over, and they came to only after the halls had cleared. He remembered a homecoming freshman year where he and another, Chad or Russell no doubt, duct-taped Darius Clark to the gazebo behind the small varsity stadium. This part came out in the papers. They found the boy the next morning with the dew clung to him like he was just some naked thing, his slender throat slit and his asshole turned inside out.

Nick watched Russell tuck a card and just looking at him Nick could tell that inside the guy's slow mind the wheels were still turning. After the conversation about payouts and percentages was all but lost he said, "It's like it was before. When Chad still came out with us." The words held a hopeful quality, excitement over the prospect of being correct.

Erik didn't answer but he didn't choke Russell either, so the conversation just died and the men continued cracking windshields and distributing the repair cards. It was a near brilliant scheme when Nick thought about it: the damage cost the consumer nothing but time. Hell, they even got a gift card as a promotion and insurance footed the bill. Work was then performed by D and D, payouts here and there. Legit. But still, in its way, little more than petty vandalism for profit.

Nick felt he was back with the boys he ran with in high school—the broken windows and tire-torn lawns of youth. Empty bottles in the backseat as they cheated death night after night. They saw the world through smoke and wet glass, colors streaked to misshapen jewels across mirrors. These were the nights he best knew Grete. And a person needed to keep that vision, if they wanted to sleep with the knowledge that their actions, though inadvertently, led to the sodomizing and murder of a peer. It was news back in ninety-three. Denis Hopeflore was arrested for the crime, or was going to be before he turned himself in, still half-dressed and bloody from the encounter.

"Did they figure it's me yet?" he said with a smile before he pulled the dead kid's cock out of his pocket and dropped it on the counter. "Personal effects?" he inquired to the horrified officer, and he added his keys to the cock pile. "Yeah?"

Little details like that made it an interesting, accessible story, and the media moved in to give Horton a quarter hour of infamy. It took hold, the tragedy of a beautiful boy; glee club standout, honor roll student, and an innocent. It didn't hurt that 100% of the population was experienced either having or not having a dick. It had the whole town of Horton glued to their sets.

But Darius was forgotten as was Horton soon after. Denis claimed all of it, but pointless rumors remained, gossip of Erik's involvement, even after justice was served. Life went on—for everyone who wasn't raped and murdered.

"I'm out of cards," Russell said. He cracked another windshield.

"Fuck it," Erik said. "I'm done. C'mon third wheel, let's get you home."

Nick sat in the back seat as the radio played low, nearly inaudible, only a hum to accompany the faint light it cast.

"How's Kimmy?" Erik said to the back of the car. He socked Russell in the arm and the man gave a little chuckle.

"I don't know. Ask her next time you see her."

"Can she talk? Or is her face wired shut?" Erik turned to Russell. "Probably why he did it, right? Shut her up." He laughed to himself and Nick caught his eye in the rear view.

"You like being her errand boy?"

Nick shrugged. "Beats some jobs I've done." He

reached into his jacket for a cigarette, lit it. "You like being his?"

"Heh. Watch it boy. You end up dead, me and Russell can put together a story easy. What you think, Russell? Want to tell Chad a story?"

Russell gave another grunting laugh. "Aw. He's all right."

Erik took a Harkins tall boy from the console, cracked it and drank. "Tommy was 'all right' too, wasn't he?"

Russell spit out his beer. "Well, not anymore." He laughed.

"No. Not anymore," Erik said.

Erik stopped the car in front of Nick's place. Nick couldn't open the door quickly enough.

"Wait," Erik said as Nick started up his drive. Nick turned around and Erik was holding cash. "Your cut of the windows."

"Keep it," Nick said.

"If Chad says pay you, I pay you." Nick looked at the money and Erik added, "I just work here. Take it."

Nick took the money. For all his talk and tough routine, Erik was as much a dog as anyone connected to Chad. Nick looked at the car as it pulled away from the curb and he remembered the last car of note that had been parked in that same spot.

The Mustang had been a gift. Before Kurt DeVries had ratted him out, he was taking in a decent salary plus what he made on the side. Things were tighter financially, with the baby coming in a month, but Nick still had a piece of his once small fortune squirreled away. He put one-hundred percent cash down in hopes to drag Grete out of her muck. He knew she loved this car, and if nothing else perhaps she'd find words for him; they hadn't said more than two words in weeks at that point. He'd take anything.

She'd never said anything about the car. She hadn't had to. He'd caught her ogling them online, and he noticed the way her head would swivel hard as they passed one on the road. It was a beautiful car and when he saw the sweet thing on the side of the road with the 'for sale' sign in the window, he knew he had to buy it. He pulled a wad of cash from his pocket, and though he'd withdrawn the full price from Horton Credit Union, Nick offered the man a thousand less than the white shoe polish on the windshield was asking. Just like that Nick bought Grete her car.

He drove the car home that afternoon. The spring air was the perfect benign cool that begged a man to lie in the grass and sleep and read. He hung his arm out the window and played with the gas and the Boss Shelby lunged forward like an animal on the attack.

Nick swelled with a real happiness he hoped was only a taste of what the future might bring. He expected no miracles. He knew it wasn't going to cure her of whatever nightmare she'd fallen into, but if it could spark a memory of when things were good, when they had love and her brain was awash in a different chemical cocktail, the antithesis of whatever nightmarish spirit she'd fallen into.

Nick called in and told voicemail not to wait up for him even though he knew it wouldn't be checked. He drove around until dark, on back roads, past old gravel pits and other ancient haunts he wanted to remember. When he finally did park the Mustang in front of the house that night, it was a struggle not to wake her. She needed sleep, so he paced around the house until the sun struck through the bay window and into his eyes, leading him to Grete's bed with the retinal burn of flashing gold fireworks that tunnel-blinded him to everything but the periphery.

She'd rolled over with a flat look and clear eyes and it struck Nick how old she was, as if she'd been away and he only now was seeing her again. He wondered if he looked older to her.

"Come outside with me," Nick said. "I've got something for you."

She rolled over. "I don't want anything."

"Baby, please. You'll love it. I swear."

Her voice began to choke up. "If I come will you leave me alone?"

Those words dug out his guts but he shook off the slight. She was sick. "Okay," he said.

He'd led her outside, thought of trying to cover her eyes but thought better of it and simply pulled her gently by the rigid hand into the front yard. She saw the car and he released her. She took two steps forward and stopped.

"What is this?" she said.

"It's your Boss," he said. "I got it for you."

Grete shuddered and Nick knew she was crying and he put a hand on her shoulder which she ripped off and slapped him hard across the neck and again in the chest. He stepped back and she fell to the ground. Nick knelt beside her and she began slapping at him again. He jumped back.

"What the hell is the matter?" he said.

Her belly quivered and her eyes found him with more interest than he could remember in a very long time.

"How did my Dad die?" she said.

"In a wreck," Nick said. His mouth betrayed his disappointment and annoyance until he puzzled together what that could possibly have to do with the beautiful automobile in front of their house.

"I didn't know. I'm sorry. I just. Jesus, I'm sorry, Grete."

She looked at him with eyes that wanted to slay him but couldn't raise the effort. She collapsed into a sobbing, pregnant heap, shaking under her cotton robe. Neighbors poked their heads out to see what the commotion was about and Nick felt their eyes. He looked closer at the car and saw the windshield was cracked on the driver's side and he could see her father's car superimposed over hers, crushed and tree warped as the man was thrown through the glass.

Two days later Grete started up the Shelby again, pulled it into the garage, and closed herself in. And that's where Nick found her hours later.

Nick continued to stare at the empty space in front of his home, and a small detail he'd forgotten nagged at him. He entered the garage and stepped to the car, pulled off the cover. He stared for a long time at the crack in the windshield. Nick pulled the card from under the windshield, an older, cruder version of the card, the name and number of the service handwritten. But the name was the same, D and D Glass. It made him realize that everything set into motion was a long time coming. It was inevitable in a place like Horton, the price you paid to stay.

***

Nick watched the taillights until they were gone and walked to the door. It was open a crack. Nick shook his head, fucking tired of the shit and just tired in general. He opened the door to find Kimmy at the kitchen table. She held a bottle of Boone's Farm kid-friendly wine and a six pack of High Life. Double fisting it, glassy eyed and gabby.

"Hi! Welcome to your home."

Nick didn't shut the door. "You need to go. Get."

"I can't drive," she smiled. "You aren't going to let me drive, are you?"

"Where's your car? I'll drive you."

She slumped in her seat, not hurt but coolly resigned. She cocked a smile that was mostly just annoyed. "Not a bit of fun are you, Gillis?"

***

Her car was two blocks over. Nick stopped as he approached the slumping vehicle.

"You got a flat."

"Yeah. I forgot to tell you."

"Spare?" Nick asked. She shook her head. He had her keys so he opened the trunk for himself. There was the spare and Nick was ready to call her out on the lie, but this tire was also flat, chewed-up steel belts spilling from the rubber like scratching, tetanus-laced tentacles.

Nick slammed the trunk. "Let's go. I'll walk you." He started off and waited for her to protest or further stall him, but heard only the clicking of her feet as she caught up.

"How long's it going to take?" she asked.

"A while. You know, if you'd just stayed home you'd be there already."

He took the remainder of the six pack from her hand and cracked one to kill time and lighten his load. The pair trekked the roads around the muck fields and the smell of onions was strong in the warm air.

"What did you and Chad talk about?" Kimmy said.

"Nothing much. Bowling. We bowled."

"You his friend now?"

"That bother you?"

She didn't answer and Nick thought she was considering it, or withholding, but he turned to find her sucking out the last of the wine. "No. Give me a beer," she said. "He took me to lunch the other day. To say sorry he said, but he talked about you the whole time. I think he likes you," she teased.

"He thinks I can make him money."

"He can make money. Doesn't need you. He wants a bro."

"He's got those."

"He thinks they're retards," she said with a belch. "Just high school buddies, you know? But they do what he says. He says 'jump,' they say 'into which pile of shit?' I bet they didn't even talk any shit while you were out smashing fucking windows. Am I right? You ever meet a couple of dumb asses like that didn't talk shit about the guy they work for? They're no better than his dogs."

At her door she turned to him. "There's a bottle inside. You want to come in, Nick? You want to come inside?" She let the empty Boone's Farm fall from her hand.

It hit the porch with a muted clink.

"No thanks."

She opened the door to the long hall and looked over her shoulder. "See you early?"

"For?"

"You'll see. Just get me early. Eight."

NINE

"I NEED YOU to run me to the campus," Kimmy said. "I got class in fifteen minutes. And then I need to you to stop at the vet for me. Pick up some dead dogs for my art installation."

Nick shook his head, incredulous. Two hours this morning dealing with Kimmy's tires and now this. "Art installation? Un-fucking-believable! You're going to get me killed by your man, and what do I have to show for it? Art made of dead dogs."

Kimmy leaned to Nick, too close. "First off, he isn't my man, no matter what he says. I don't belong to anybody but my girl. And second, you aren't going to get killed. Chief told us what we needed to do and that's what we're going to do. I need you to get me to school and then get to the vet and I promise you things are going to work out just fine." Kimmy squeaked as she tried to turn to him, her head still caught in the grips of the halo. "Fuck this! Pull over."

Nick hesitated but did as she asked. The tires hit the gravel shoulder with the sound of popcorn popping and a dust cloud engulfed the car before clearing with the breeze. His resignation bothered him and it made him think about his wife, the things she asked him to do that he always did. Made him remember how he stopped doing things. And what that led to.

Kimmy got out of the car. "Pop the trunk," she said. She came back moments later, took her place in the passenger seat, and handed Nick a small screwdriver. Nick's eyes moved from the tool to her face, then to the screws attaching the metal to her skull.

"No," he said. "You're going to break your neck."

"It was barely fractured, doc said. Do it or I'll just do it myself anyway."

And Nick found himself leaning into her, finding the head of each screw and twisting, torqueing each loose and eliciting a small gasp from the patient. As each screw fell away, the holes left behind slowly filled with blood. She wept softly. And when he finished, she pulled the headgear from her body and tossed it away into the tall grass, moving her head slowly from side to side, cautiously testing her freedom. She got back into the car.

"Now let's fucking go," she said.

***

Nick pulled up to the curb of Grand Rapids

Community College, the same school he'd attended after getting kicked out of State. It had been some years but it hadn't changed at all. He watched Kimmy walk to the door, barely a limp left and looking almost herself from behind. She turned before entering the glass doors, smiling like the Ottawa Indian woman in the mural over the door. It was an Ottawa creation story: the towering female figure sat on the bank of the tiny Thornapple River, using a piece of native pottery, not collecting water but pouring, supplying the river with moisture and fish and beaver, each gift depicted within the flowing, blue, painted water.

Kimmy disappeared inside and Nick pulled away. He was still irritated and, in truth, scared. Kimmy could give him all the guarantees in the world but it didn't mean anything. How seriously could he take her? She was planning a murder and in the same breath planning a community college art project. Unfucking believable.

From behind, she looked like the girl he remembered. Her legs were tan and smooth, and Nick thought about such stems wrapped around him, squeezing, choking the life out of him. He didn't want to die, but what a way to go. *Don't fuck my goat.*

Nick pulled into the lot of Every Creature's Animal Hospital, approached the delivery door, and rang the bell. After a moment the security door adjacent to the bay door cracked open and a Hispanic guy with a shaved head, early twenties, popped his dome out of the doorway and eyeballed Nick.

"Dog guy?" he said after a moment.

"I suppose," Nick answered.

The guy offered a nod and opened the bay door. Nick stepped inside the storage area of the clinic, followed the guy past stacked-to-the-ceiling bags of specialty dog foods, organic toys, and flea treatments. The back of the guy's bald head was tattooed with a green outline of the state of Texas. The form was blank except for "El Paso" in black script, and the city's precise location marked with a small red rose. Nick continued following through the kennels and through a dark hallway where El Paso dipped his feet into a cat litter box containing a frothy white chemical mixture.

"Dip your feet and follow me," El Paso said.

Nick dipped and followed into the small room. The stench of sweet death was foul and assaulting.

"Parvo," El Paso said before Nick could ask. El Paso pointed to a small cage and a fluffy brown puppy inside. The thing looked miserable, shivering with fever under the blanket and heat bottle, tiny leg affixed with an IV needle of hydrating fluids. "Whole litter of 7 came in with it," he continued. "She's the last."

El Paso opened the large freezer. Inside Nick saw various amorphous bundles of heavy brown plastic. On top of the pile were six tiny packages, the size of a drive-thru burrito. The kid pushed the small bundles aside, leaned deep inside and came out with a grunt-worthy bundle in his arms, this one large and wrapped in the same heavy plastic as the pups. El Paso grunted again as the weight shifted. "Grab the other one, huh?"

Nick stepped inside the door and at the opposite end of the large storage room, past shelves of specialty dog foods and tartar fighting chew toys and flea treatments was the freezer. The top was open and inside Nick found a package similar to the one the kid had just brought out. Nick grabbed it. It was heavy, frozen solid. Nick struggled with the grip, propping it on one end, giving it a hug, and lifting it from the cold box. Inside the plastic was a single frozen form and, though the end was taped shut, a hairy canine tail poked out of a gap.

Nick lugged the package to the car and dropped it in the open trunk on top of the other package. Nick followed El Paso back inside and repeated the drill five more times. As Nick was stuffing the last of the carcasses into the car, he was sure this had to be some terrible delusion brought on by psychosis.

"Phenobarbital? Propofol?" El Paso said.

"Morphine? Ketamine? What else you need?"

"I'm good," Nick said.

"He's good." El Paso laughed. "Right on. You know anybody wants a party, you send them this way."

"You bet," Nick said, and started the car. He pulled away and watched in the rearview as the guy watched him drive away. The icy dogs shifted in the trunk and back seats as Nick pulled out of the lot. Nick could only imagine the art project Kimmy had planned. Dead dogs. Art? Nick couldn't judge. Either all of it was or none of it was. Nick preferred to think that all of it was. Otherwise it was just a bunch of assholes doing shit.

***

The one positive thing about hauling not one, not two, but thirteen dead dogs through the cornfield across the stream and into the clearing Kimmy had made, was that for the time Nick sweated and exerted himself and hated dogs in general, he forgot about hating other things. He even forgot for a time that his death was almost certainly imminent. But his mental vacation was cut short as the damp heat hung in the air, an oppressive pressure, and Nick knew the only way to escape it was to get out. Leave.

He could run. Why wouldn't he run? Nothing keeping him in Horton, nothing but his bullshit situation. And he entertained that thought, but Kimmy kept coming back to him. She was the reason he couldn't leave. And he wasn't overlooking the tape. He was trying not to factor it in, taking it for granted that Chief wouldn't give chase.

Nick wiped the sweat from his brow. It was early but hot, the moist air blowing in from Lake Michigan, warming and thickening and creating a wet, breathable soup that pulled the moisture from his body, then left it to sit. Nick moved to the edge of the clearing and sat in the dirt on the short shade of the eastern tree line. The sun was almost directly overhead and cool space was at a premium. Nick caught his breath in the shade and the breeze did its best to wipe away the sweat and hot. He dragged a dirty arm across his forehead. He eyed the plastic wrapped art supplies in the middle of the clearing. Dead animals as art. He didn't know what to make of it, didn't want to know *anything* anymore.

With rest came clarity and the things he had been able to forget came back and he hated Hobo for being dead and making him feel like he owed him something. It was Hobo that had pulled *him* into this pile of shit sandwiches. Choices. And again his mind went to Kimmy. Was she even worth protecting? The fight in her was, he saw it, the way she pummeled the blonde with the cue ball. If she brought the same fight to her plan for Chad, Nick wasn't sure she wouldn't just pull it off. The fight was her strength and her liability, but regardless, she was the type to go until she had what she wanted. And in that spirit Nick found the part of her worth saving. He'd signed on when he got into her car that night. He'd signed on for better or worse with an act of kindness. And it would certainly kill him.

He walked slowly through the corn. He saw no crows but felt their curious eyes. Nick grabbed at the stalks he passed, choking and shaking them to life with a sound like television static. But it was about as entertaining as one would expect, and Nick thought about Kimmy and her girl, and her story of the Scarecrow Man. Her life was the Scarecrow Man, it takes and takes, always with a promise to return what it's borrowed, but it never will. Its promises are addict-honesty, empty words spoken to further its own agenda, despite the sincerity in its eyes.

Nick found Kimmy on the porch before she saw him. She was sitting in the sunshine and dragging her toes in the hard dirt of the worn path leading to the stairs. Her smile was simple and true and it was easy to see her as a child. Then he saw her legs and he hated himself for seeing them, and he saw her growing up against a backdrop of beauty and lust and sin. He wondered how a pretty girl makes sense of the lechery she faces every day, how once-kind eyes turn as they notice what a "fine young woman she's becoming," as those eyes find her in the dark, especially in the dark, and turn her into something else, an object to be enjoyed. And she *is* enjoyed. The curse of every beautiful girl. And add the desire to please, the need to be wanted when you're not. It's a fucking tightrope Nick could never know. And he hated that he was looking and wanted her. Except the part of him that loved it.

Kimmy looked up from her shoes.

"How'd you get here?" he said.

"Mama. She and Janie picked me up and we went to McDonald's."

"Thought you were on the outs," Nick said. "Don't come back and that?"

Kimmy shrugged. "She doesn't mean it." She thought about that and laughed. "Maybe she does, but she can't stick by it. It's her way. She takes things in, men mostly, but she feeds the crows, takes care of my girl while I can't."

Nick looked at the house. The sun was mercifully below the corn and Nick could see the house was dark. No car but his in the drive.

"Where are they now?"

"Gone. For the weekend. I got to get a couple things. Want to come inside?"

"Nah. Just grab whatever it is and we'll go."

"I need you to carry it. Just come in and see the place I came from."

Inside, the trailer smelled of cinnamon and dust. The place was cluttered with country knick-knacks and dolls, hundreds of dolls among old-fashioned butter churns and wooden rocking chairs. Cross-stitch needlework served as art, crowded on tables and other surfaces, framed like family photos. No real people were in any of the frames, only more dolls and country life vistas made of fabric and thread.

Kimmy turned on the lights and the fully mirrored walls of the living room reflected the scene to infinity. Nick followed Kimmy to the small kitchen. She grabbed a can of beer from the refrigerator and handed it to Nick. Then she pulled out a half full container of orange juice and added the remains of a vodka bottle. She swirled the mix and took a drink from the carton.

"C'mon," she said. "I want to show you something."

Nick followed her down the dark hall and eyed the photos on the wall. "Where'd they go?" he said as he straightened a photograph of Kimmy.

"Gone to Goshen, Indiana. Annual trip with my

aunt. They like the Amish pies."

Nick followed Kimmy into a small, child's bedroom, her daughter's. She took a seat on the unmade bed and patted the place next to her. "Sit." Nick downed his beer and set the empty can on the white dresser next to a snow globe. Inside the glass sphere was a plastic barn-raising scene with plastic Amish men wearing plastic beards, frozen as they hammered and hoisted.

Nick took a seat and Kimmy leaned forward, reached under the bed and retrieved a photo album. She opened it and started looking through the pages. She didn't say anything and Nick sat quietly, wishing he had another beer to keep him occupied. He looked over as she flipped through Christmases, summer scenes at a brown lake, birthdays, New Years. She stopped on a photo of a young girl sitting on the knee of a mustached man wearing a Pabst Blue Ribbon hat to match the can in his hand. She lingered.

"Who's that?" Nick asked. "Your pop?"

"Nope. Uncle Todd. Not really my uncle. Boyfriend of my mom."

"You guys close?"

"We were. Till I got older." She left it at that and walked away. Nick remained in the small, crowded living room until she came back from the hall, grabbed him by the arm, and dragged him behind her.

The doll eyes followed him everywhere.

She led him to a small pink bedroom. The walls were decorated with unicorn posters and drawings of animals, mostly elephants, a few crows on power lines like the ones that ran in front of the house, outside the fields. Kimmy kneeled in the small bed and reached between the mattress and box spring. She retrieved a photo, looked at it for only a few seconds before the emotion was too much. She lay the photo on the bed. It was her, younger, but still the beauty she was holding a boy a little older than her.

Nick asked the only question that came to mind given the company she kept. "Where is he?"

"Prison." She choked before tamping her sorrow down with a hard sigh. "Way up in Iron Mountain. Been there about seven years."

She picked up the photo again. She cried softly at first, then she was sobbing. Before Nick could put an arm around her, Kimmy leaned into him, sobbing into his t-shirt.

"It's okay," he said.

She recoiled. "It isn't! It's shit! All of it is shit! He's never coming back to me. I loved him! We were going to leave this place and never come back. But look at me, still here! Can't even take care of my girl!" She shook hard and fell into Nick again. "I got to get her out of this place, Nick! He's going to put his mitts all over my baby!"

"Who is?" Nick asked.

Kimmy pulled away. "Whoever it is that wants to. And mama's going to let him because that's the price you pay to have a man in the house!"

And then she was calm, spent, like a little kid who doesn't know how tired they are until they collapse. She hugged Nick, and Nick held her and looked around the room. So much pink. Everywhere.

"That's why I need to get her out, Nick. That's why." She ran out of words and Nick held on to her, stroked the tear-dampened hair from her face. She burrowed in deeper and it hit Nick the kind of damage a man can do. And how a girl can grow up seeking out the very thing she should avoid.

"I'm sorry," she told his chest, her voice muffled, vibrating against him. "I didn't want this to happen. I just want my baby." He pulled her tighter and she continued to cry. He felt better than he had in a long time. His own demons could sleep while he was dealing with hers. But even the relief nagged at him. Was it worth it? Leave one hell to vacation in another? And how long until he had to go back home?

Ten

THE BLACK FORD cut through the night. Chad maneuvered the truck in and out of traffic deftly. He was alert, reminded Nick of a cocky pilot out of some 1980s action film, jetting through hostile territory on the way to get the bad guy.

"I'm really looking forward to this, Nick," Chad said. "I gotta tell you."

They were alone again, aside from the dogs behind them in the extended cab. Nick had no idea what Chad had planned this evening; the man was nothing if not unpredictable. Nick *did* know that at the end of the night he could be dog food or he could have a pocket full of cash. Nick figured whatever tone the evening took, the piece would be useful. But despite some ambiguity, there was a crystal clear truth—Chad had taken some sort of shine to him. But then, that shine had also lit up Kimmy bright as the sun.

"Where we going?" Nick asked.

"You'll see." Chad stepped on the gas and the truck picked up speed. "Got to step on it. We're on a timer."

"Where's Erik and Russell?"

"Relax with the questions, huh?" Chad said. So Nick did and neither of them spoke until they hit the eastbound I-96 north toward Grand Rapids.

Nick pulled a pack of cigarettes from his pocket, ripped it open and put one in his mouth. Chad held out his hand so Nick coughed up another. "Light me up," Chad said and Nick did. Then he lit his own and let the cellophane fly free as he cracked open the window.

"I love her. You know that, right?"

"You say so," Nick said. He kept looking forward, felt Chad trying to size him up again, like the night on the boat.

"There's honesty in you." Chad grinned. "Even if it is a bit sarcastic. College does that to people, makes them sarcastic, cynical. Dad told me that. Smacked me sideways the couple times he caught me reading something from the library. Wasn't too appreciative of education, my old man."

Nick thought for a moment. "I don't know. He's not altogether wrong. The more you know," Nick took a long drag from his cigarette and tossed it out the window, "the more you know you don't."

Chad thought on that one, then gave Nick an appreciative nod. "This. This is why Erik and Russell aren't with us. I can't have a conversation like this with them. They got nothing to offer on anything except NASCAR and TV, cartoons mostly. I don't like that shit, never have."

Chad changed lanes and took the 196 east. The on-ramp curved sharp and inertia pulled everyone, dogs included, to the left until the road finally straightened. Chad gunned the truck hard down the merge lane, passing a long line of cars before cutting over.

"I've always loved that girl. She tell you we grew up together?"

"No. I didn't know that."

"She was always a fucking knockout. Even back then." Chad looked over to Nick. "That was a bad thing to be with her mom. With the men she brought home."

Nick offered a 'Hm' in response. He didn't particularly care to hear this information. But Chad wanted to talk in a way he hadn't been able to, it seemed, in a very long time. And Nick was his captive audience.

"Hm," Chad echoed. "You said it. A lot of it going on. I was too young to do anything about it, and she promised me to keep quiet. I did. But it wasn't for her. It was for me. I knew another kid from school whose sister was taken away for someone diddling her. And I didn't want her to go, you know? So I kept it to myself, but I'd still lay awake at night, wonder if she was hurting right then. Wonder what I could do about it, not able to do a damn thing."

Nick shifted in his seat, wished there were some kind of confessional mesh between them. He felt the hot breath of one of the dogs as it sniffed at his collar. It made his hair stand on end. The radio was lit bright on the dash, a custom deck glowing in orange and blue. The volume was down to zero so it offered no relief from the silence. The silence itself wasn't the problem, it was that the meant more talk was inevitable.

The truck glided off the highway alone and merged into the light traffic over the six lanes that made up Twenty-eighth Street. Though they weren't that far from Horton, ten miles perhaps, Nick realized he hadn't been out of the city limits proper in a very long time. The city looked familiar, but as if he'd only remembered it from a movie. He tried to see himself inside the bars and restaurants and stores that lined the street, places he'd been before fatherhood and responsibility. But it wasn't him. It was a character who looked like him. With Grete. Was that even her name? Nick felt he was in a dream he wouldn't wake from, and that inability to wake was what made it his nightmare. Nick asked himself how far back the nightmare went. Did it begin with losing his job? Death? Kimmy Flynn's thighs?

They approached the neon glow of the crowded DeAnza Drive-In. The marquee glowed bright: THE LA5T PICTUR SHOW THANKS FOR THE MEMORYS

"Last show and then they close forever," Chad said. "Perfect movie, right?"

Nick hadn't been to the drive-in in years, didn't know it was still open. He wondered what they were actually there for. "C'mon, tell me what's up?"

Chad leaned close into the wheel, trying to see everything around the truck. He honked the horn as three teenage girls stumbled across the dirt drive to the concession stand. All three jumped then laughed and moved their too-young legs through the dusty cloud of dirt raised by the rumbling Ford.

"We're going to see a movie, buddy. One of my favorites. And I chose to bring you with me, over every other person I know because I think you'll appreciate it. Satisfied? It's a friendly night out. Got something to do afterward, but for now let's just pretend we're friends with something in common, huh?"

Ushers with air traffic control wands directed the traffic toward available spaces. Chad was sent left, where he joined a row of too-tall vehicles, trucks like Chad's, boxy SUVs of crying kids, a full-size van with, no doubt, converted beds behind the bead and macramé curtains.

Chad turned off the vehicle and sat staring at the empty white screen of the DeAnza. On either side of the forty-foot screen, a classic cartoon character peeked out at the people in the lot. On the left was an approximation of Disney's Goofy. On the right it was an equally malformed Daffy Duck. Both had been defiled with spray paint—giant erect penises added to their charm.

Chad reached under the seat and pulled out two cold tall boys and a pint of Maker's. He tossed a beer to Nick, uncapped the whiskey, took a pull then handed the pint over. Nick took a swallow and handed it back before taking down a long chaser of watery beer.

"I'm going to tell you a story. You want to know about the last time I was here?"

"Sure." Nick took another drink from his can. He looked out the passenger window, his body language practically repelling the chance for conversation. Behind the men, the dogs had settled into licking themselves.

"I told you I loved her always. When we were thirteen I took her here. Saved up my money, got an older kid to give us a ride. I was going to tell her that I loved her. Well, the thirteen-year-old version of it anyway. I even brought us a blanket to set out on."

Chad pointed up to another small rise where young couples lay under the stairs, waiting for the movie to begin. Some were kissing, some barely daring to let their hands touch, some fearing nothing.

"It was the middle of the movie and I heard these voices coming up the rise. They were loud. They came to us and sat with us, got in close and they smelled of alcohol. 'What are you doing with this asshole' they said to her. I didn't know what to say. I was just a little shit and they were three kids old enough to get drunk and fuck with little shits. One of them started asking a lot of questions of Kimmy. Where she was from? Where she went to school? If she knew so and so? I figured I had to say something so I said, 'This is a date, guys. Can you leave us alone?' There was a silence and I thought, man, maybe that's all there is to it, but it wasn't. 'This a date?' the one talking to her asked. She didn't answer. She didn't have to. He moved in and gave Kimmy the kiss on the mouth that was supposed to be mine. 'Don't look like no date to me,' one of his buddies goes. And then the pair of them dragged me off the hill. I called after her but she kept on lip smacking with that boy, ignoring me, and that's the last I saw of her that night. I was stupid enough to think maybe she'd just been scared. I hoped she wasn't going to get the same as I was, which was my ass stomped behind the concession building. I didn't even know those guys. After they were done with me, we were close though. You think Kimmy looked bad? Shit. Dad's the only one to see me in the hospital. Asked if I knew who did it. Told him no. I knew he'd take care of it if I told him, and I didn't want that. I was going to get it, myself.

"Kimmy never came to see how I was. Next time I saw her that kissing boy was picking her up from her mom's in his shitty Camaro." Chad stroked the gleaming steering wheel in the dark, loving it like it was proof of his own worth. "She made her choice. Found her a man she wanted. Didn't matter to her mom that he was twenty years old. I mean, the girl didn't even have tits until the summer before! But that was old enough as far as she was concerned." Chad drained his can and took another pull from the whiskey. "You remember that story, okay? Movie's starting." And upon the screen appeared the words: The Last Picture Show, in big white letters on black. And the black faded into a street—bleak and grit covered. The camera panned across the dusty, windblown street, from one side to the other over a virtual ghost town.

"Jeff Bridges is in this, you know that?" Chad said.

"I didn't," Nick said. "Must have been young."

"Shh. Shut up. There he is."

***

It was after 2 AM when the last car pulled out of the lot, leaving only Nick and Chad and the dogs. Chad removed the borrowed speaker from his window, let it drop. He turned the vehicle around in a quick reverse U that had Nick grabbing for the 'oh shit' handle. Chad revved the engine in neutral and threw it into gear. The truck stomped forward, over the speaker boxes on their wood posts, making as the crow flies toward the concessions and theater offices, splinters flying off the titanium grill of the truck. Just shy of the front door he cut left and stopped fast, nose end toward the open gate.

"Let's go, boys," Chad said.

Nick opened his door while wondering if he meant him and the dogs or just the dogs. He figured he wasn't there for his looks and was glad for the piece, though he hoped he wouldn't have to pull it out let alone use it.

He followed Chad and the dogs through the door and into the brightly lit lobby. Three men looked up from behind the glass counter. They were gorging themselves on Chuckles and Milk Duds as the popcorn machine did its thing behind them. The Cure's "Boys Don't Cry" played tinny on the AM/FM/8-Track mounted on the wall beneath a

Coca-Cola brand clock/menu board.

The one in the middle was full of girth and gray, and he looked at them with loud white eyes that bugged out to half orbs resting in the black soup of the sockets. He smiled and his teeth were yellow with neglect and red with jelly candy.

"Chad. Who's the friend?"

"It's Nick, but don't worry about that." Chad rubbed his dogs behind the ears, but they didn't take their eyes off the man in the middle. He backed up from his counter slouch and rested his ass on the counter behind him. His boys did the same, though their eyes were less calm as they looked at Chad and the beasts. Chad didn't seem interested in them, keeping his eyes on the man between them. No one spoke for a long time until finally, the middle boy shrugged. "Damn busy night. If they'd have shown up in half these numbers in the past we wouldn't be shutting down." His posture loosened and he shook his head, still smiling.

"Ain't that something," Chad said. It was quiet again.

Nick felt the pull of his piece, almost in connection to the gray boy's movement. He stood back watching the scene play out in slow motion, then he was eyeing the back of Chad's head. One shot. Then unload on the dogs. He could make it out the door with three witnesses to animal cruelties and a murder two, and that was if he made it before that old boy found whatever he was reaching for.

Nick pulled and cocked the piece so quick even the dogs flinched, but the boy held still, arm dangling lower.

"He's going for something."

The boy panicked and stood tall, hands up. "I don't have shit!"

"Don't you?" Chad said. "Move. You two boys, come around where we can see you. Then I'm going to have a conversation with your friend. Nick, shoot them if they try to get cute." Chad stepped back to allow the two men out from behind the glass to the small lobby. Chad pointed the them to a small table for two near the window. "You boys got anything?"

Each of them patted themselves down and shook their heads. They were a pair. It was only then that Nick took them for twins, fat and squat twins, both with a haircut like a plate of scrambled eggs. One wore a beard and the other thick glasses tinted rose.

"We're just here on business," the bearded one said.

"Me too," said Chad. "What's your business?"

The bearded twin looked at his brother and continued to speak for them both. "We're buying the drive-in."

"Chad, your business was with my dad, not me. I can give you a cut of what we took tonight, but I just can't pay out. You know that. How many times you talked to my old man?"

"More times than I should have," Chad said. "But he's dead and this place is yours and we do indeed have business. But probably not what you're thinking. I'll take that cut and then some, but I was ready to call it a wash." Chad's eyes found the twins. "This deal go through?" The twin with the glasses nodded and his brother punched him in the cock for it. Chad smiled. "We'll talk soon, give you time to set up shop. Got some speaker poles need fixed."

"Can we go?"

"No," Chad said. "You need to see this." "What do you think this old boy's name is, Nick?"

"I don't know," Nick said.

"Have a guess!" Chad said, smiling.

"Mud."

"Ha! You'd think. And maybe. But this thing goes by the name of Billy Ray. How about that? A real good ol' boy. Aren't you, Billy Ray?" Billy Ray said nothing. "He's a bit shy, wants to downplay it, how much of a redneck motherfucker he is." Chad's smile left and his eyes grew cold, skipping the calm-eyed sizing up Nick had seen for himself.

"Billy Ray the name on your birth certificate?"

Chad asked. "Please tell me your dad had the decency to make it William on the dotted line. Fucking Billy Ray!" Chad turned to Nick. "Remember the story I told you in the truck tonight? About me and Kimmy and what happened when we came here last?" He didn't wait for Nick to answer. "This is one of the two sons of bitches worked me over. The other one died in a car wreck, not a week later, didn't he? You know, Billy Ray, I remember seeing the news and wondering why it wasn't you. Why do you suppose I'd think like that, Nick? Both boys were responsible for putting me in the hospital. Why do you think I'd rather see this one dead?"

"Couldn't say," Nick said. "Or did you want me to guess?"

"You remember, Billy Ray? You do. You remember that night. After we left Tommy alone with Kimmy. Remember? You're getting hard just thinking about it."

The gun lowered in Nick's hand, pointed at the boy's heavy belly hanging over his belt buckle. He knew he wouldn't have to shoot him. Whatever he'd done had warranted a wrath far beyond that of tag-along muscle. As if reading his mind, the boy looked at the dogs.

"The other boy, he beat on me and left. But you stayed. Didn't you?"

The man nodded. "I stayed back."

"And did what?"

The man shook his head. Defiant as a man can be at his certain demise. "I stirred your little pot."

"How many other pots you stirred the years your dad ran this place?"

He shook his head again, laughed lightly and looked up from the floor to meet Chad's eye. "I played some games but nothing like with you. You were the sweet one. And we only had the once. I prayed, honest to God prayed that you'd be stupid enough to come back. I waited for you." The man smiled. "That sweet boy's face the one I call on when I can't do it for my lady." Chad remained silent, showed nothing and had nothing but the dogs.

"So let 'em eat me. I heard what you do. You know what I'm going to be thinking about."

Chad looked disappointed. In himself or the man? Probably both as final confrontations go. The guilty defiant, meeting his end on his own terms. But what the defiant Billy Ray didn't count on was surviving.

"Think about whatever you like," Chad said. Then, "Fuck him, boys." And Nick saw, before common sense overtook initial shock, that the dogs were as well trained as Kimmy's crows, biting and mounting Billy Ray on both ends, chewing and ripping apart the man's cock as they raped him.

Nick stumbled out of the concession stand with the twins on his heels. The muffled squeals and growls were little relief from the act. Soon it quieted and was little more than crying. Chad stepped out with a bag of cash, the take, and tossed it into Nick's arms. "Get in," he said. "They're near finished."

Nick looked in the open bag and it looked like what it was said to be, the take of the drive in, crumpled small bills mostly, not much more than burning money for Chad Toll. But it was the principle of the thing. You had to take everything that mattered, let a man keep his life. Especially if it belonged to you anyway.

Chad jumped into the driver's side and soon enough the dogs trotted out. Nick realized his missed opportunity and how long of a timeline he and Chief were working with. Chad pressed buttons on the dash steering column and the truck's suicide back door opened behind Nick and the dogs.

He pulled away from the drive-in. A moment later the smell crept up on them. Chad lowered the windows and laughed. "Jesus Christ!" he said. "I'd tell you that he'd be fine but my god! Get that man to the ass doc because he's got something dead up there! Or did you get it for him, boys?"

Soon the smell was gone but the air had become cold and biting. Nick tried in vain to light a cigarette before tossing the wind broken tobacco stick out the window.

"Need you to do something in a couple days!" Chad yelled over the wind. "You're taking Kimmy up to Iron Mountain."

"What's in Iron Mountain?"

"You'll just see!" Chad said, then out the window, to the heavens. "You'll just see!"

They drove and Nick thought about the crime, what the older boys, men, had done to Chad. In the end the knowledge was nothing more than more liability. Chad Toll had been keeping a dark secret for a very long time. But now he was free, having Nick as a witness to his revenge, to carry the burden of what had happened those years ago.

Nick worked on another cigarette, cupping his hand against the wind. Chad didn't need to tell him. He knew damn well what was waiting in Iron Mountain. He was going to meet the boy that ruined Chad's life.

The lighter sparked to life long enough to breathe death into Nick's lungs. Before he could take a real drag Chad plucked it out of his fingers and put it to his own lips.

Eleven

THE FIRST PART of the Kurt DeVries job was easy enough to figure out; Nick had all the contraband he needed growing in his basement. He retrieved an ounce of a strong sativa from the basement and when he returned to the main level of the house, Kimmy was waiting at the kitchen table, a glass of water and a sleeve of crackers in front of her.

"I'm busy," Nick said.

"Doing what?" she asked. She didn't look at him, just stared into the sleeve of square crackers as if they held all the answers. Nick took a seat at the table and looked at her glassy eyes. She looked up at him for a moment before finding the water glass and downing it in a series of long gulps that spilled water from the corners of her mouth and down her chin, spotting her pink shirt and cleavage.

"What are you on?"

She laughed. "Does it matter?"

Nick ignored the question and took her glass as she nibbled on a cracker. He moved to the kitchen, filled the glass from the sink and put it in front of her. He took his seat. She sniffed, smiling as she smelled the aroma of the illicit buds wafting from his jacket pocket.

"Thought you didn't smoke."

He didn't answer and Kimmy continued staring at the water glass, nibbling a cracker and dropping crumbs on the table. He resented her and cared for her at the same time. He knew it wasn't love in any real sense, nothing more than run of the mill suppressed lust coupled with projected guilt, twisted and spun around. A little bit processed, like factory food enriched with additives that addicted him to her taste, her company.

His gaze drifted to her smooth legs and back up to her face. The swelling was going down, her screw holes had been cleaned and she smelled sweet like the strippers he remembered from his Las Vegas bachelor party, like candy. He breathed her in despite himself. Closing his eyes, the candy and cannabis together put him in a youthful place.

"You coming with me?" he sighed.

***

It felt good to be on the course again, better than he'd have thought. Even with Kimmy tagging along, Nick felt good. And he did take a certain pleasure in forcing Kimmy to help him lug the twenty-pound salt bags from the trunk. They headed to the fence line closest to the eighth hole, near the pond.

"What's Chad got you doing?" she grunted. "Thought we were dropping off a little pot."

"That too," Nick said. "This is for me though."

Nick tried to hold onto the feeling though it threatened him with its own kind of suicide. He liked to think that past and present criminal activity aside, he was the decent person people saw. Someone who didn't cause trouble, didn't want it. Someone who wouldn't do dirt at the behest of someone else, especially if the dirt meant fucking over someone who didn't deserve it. Did Kurt DeVries deserve what he was doing to him? In certain circles, prison maybe, he'd be a snitch bitch who'd gotten what he deserved a long time ago. He'd been pining for Nick's job, said as much. The right thing done for the wrong reasons is like a contract signed under duress. Doesn't mean shit. That's what Nick told himself. So he gave in to the personal pleasure it was going to give him to fuck over Kurt Devries. Get him locked up, miss the bowling finals, petty shit. Nick was sure he'd walk away from the ordeal unscathed. And that's what the salt was for.

Nick and Kimmy moved quickly in the dark. Kimmy attempted to hoist the bags over the fence, but her throws fell short each time. "Fuck it!" she said.

Nick laughed. "And fuck you!" she added before leaving the bag on the ground for Nick to retrieve. She disappeared into the dark tree line that separated the road from the tall chain link. Nick was ready to write off her help, but as he hoisted her bag over the fence she came out of the trees with two more. She dropped them at his feet as he reached out for them, then disappeared again.

"This is the last of them," she said when she returned again, huffing and glowing, wet in the moonlight. Nick had liked the idea of taking a little revenge on the girl for all the sweating she'd had him doing. But whatever she was into this evening had her in good spirits. Nick liked to think maybe it was bringing out the real Kimmy, or if it was what she was on, at least it made her better company.

"Now what?" She grinned, teeth clenched.

"Now we hop the fence," Nick said. "That going to be a problem?"

She answered by scrambling up the chain link and hoisting herself over with an ease she hadn't been able to muster for the bags. Nick took a look over his shoulder before following.

"C'mon," Nick said.

"What about the salt?" she asked.

"Leave it. We've got something else to do first."

The fairway leading up to the clubhouse was well

lit. Giant spots hummed with power and swarms of tiny nighttime bugs clicked their hard bodies together as they flew in confused, overlapping patterns. Nick and Kimmy hung close to the shadowy rough, made their way over the hills, and finally reached the first hole and the clubhouse beyond.

"What about cameras?"

"Broken when I was here."

"So how do you know they didn't fix 'em?"

"Kurt Devries didn't replace them when I told him to. No reason to think he'd do it with no one telling him to."

Nick led Kimmy up the cobblestone path, past the small dining patio where the Mayor and Art Sojka of Sojka Chevy ate pancakes and bacon before their Friday morning eighteens. Nick skirted by the brunch steam carts tucked away in a dark corner near the building. They entered a small service corridor that descended to the basement level. Nick tried the delivery door and found it locked. Outside Swingers, the club bar and drinking patio, he jumped and swiped across the rafters. The whole place smelled of old rich piss that dripped through the wooden deck. Nick couldn't help but think about the day Paul Troost, club manager, had told him that some members were complaining about the smell and it needed to be taken care of, and the memory had him swearing under his breath as he felt in the dark and detritus for the key. His finger touched metal. Found it.

"You okay?" Kimmy said.

"Fine," Nick said. He sparked his lighter and found the key. He opened the door, ushered Kimmy inside, and closed the door gently.

Nick took a hard right at the first dark hall of the club kitchen. At the end of the hall was a large locker room with the employee time clock hanging next to the door. He flicked on the light switch as Kimmy watched him from the hall.

"The hell you doing?" she said. "Why you messing with that?"

Nick huffed with a satisfied chuckle as he located and pulled Kurt DeVries's time card from its slot next to the clock. "Because most criminals are dumb fucks," he said, punctuating the sentence with an exclamatory crunch of the time stamp. He looked at Kimmy. "Creature of habit they'll say." And he slid the card back home.

Nick pulled the ounce of weed from his pocket and opened the locker assigned to Kurt DeVries. He tucked the bag back on the top shelf of Kurt's locker.

"Oh the poor thing," Kimmy said.

Nick shot her a look. "Yeah. Poor him. Inherited the kingdom at my expense. I should have thought of this years ago." He slammed the locker. "Let's go."

Kimmy looked around the cluttered dusty space as she followed Nick out the door. "Some kingdom."

Nick started down the dark hall again to another set of doors and another dark hallway, and finally to the maintenance storage. Leaving her again in the hall, he returned pulling a gardening wagon with thick black tread tires.

"For the salt?" Kimmy said.

"For the salt. Wish we'd had one that day you had me running jars of coins back and forth."

"It would have helped."

"Yeah yeah. Make it up to me now and get a wagon," Nick said.

The wagons rumbled almost happily over the cobblestone, almost like clumsy dogs happy for fresh air. Nick left the path just beyond the first tee and Kimmy kept close behind on the way back to the place they'd come in over the fence.

After loading the wagons with the sand, Nick led the way to the large fountain pond at the eighth green. When he'd taken over, Nick had planned and oversaw the installation of a water recycling system that reclaimed runoff and clean sewer for irrigation. The project had even won the state eco award for environmental excellence the year before Nick was fired. Horton Country Club had the second largest population of threatened cricket frogs in the state, kept safe from progress by living with progress, croaking in the night in the pond where Nick and Kimmy stood.

Nick took a bag of salt, ripped it open, and poured it into the pond.

"You looking to kill the fish?" Kimmy said, handing Nick another bag.

"Not looking to, but they'll die. It's all going to die. Irrigation draws from here. Sprinklers come on in half an hour. They're going to stay on until every inch of this course is salted."

"Remind me never to get on your bad side." Kimmy tore a hole on a fresh bag and pouring it into the water. "You're too creative to say you don't enjoy it."

And Nick continued to pour sand under the moonlight and soon the croaking frogs quieted. Didn't make him happy to kill the frogs, but it had to be done. It was his own little *fuck you* to Kurt. Maybe the man deserved it, maybe he didn't.

"Everybody's done something," he thought out loud.

"Everyone's done what?" Kimmy asked.

Nick shook his head as an answer but Kimmy didn't see it. She didn't ask again. The pair just stood in the dark, pouring salt into the pond, and killing everything that depended on the fresh water

After dumping the wagons into the depths of the pond, Nick and Kimmy toted the salt bags back to the tree line. They hopped the fence again.

"Need you to drop me off at the police station," Nick said.

"What the hell you need with that son of a bitch?"

"Work stuff. Don't worry about it. Chad stuff."

She didn't say anything else on the short drive from the club to the center of Horton.

Nick got out of the car. It was still dark, going on four in the morning.

"You want me to wait for you?" Kimmy asked. She smiled but he saw how tired she was underneath it.

"Nothing worth waiting for," he said. "Get some rest. I'll see you later I'm sure."

"Chad say anything about Iron Mountain?" Kimmy said.

He nodded.

"Shit." And she drove away.

Nick climbed the steps and entered the bright lobby. He stared out the window onto the town square but saw nothing in the glass but his own reflection. And then Chief's. Nick turned with a start.

"Nervous?" Chief said. "You haven't even taken care of our problem yet? Don't need to be scared of me. Yet. Your friends on the other hand. You figure out what you're going to do about the dogs?"

"Working on it."

"Oh, I believe you. I do. But I'm the kind of man who likes to light a fire, not out of meanness or just because I can, but because I find that a man with a clock ticking in his ear is a man better able to focus on the job at hand. Forty-eight hours." Chief moved toward Nick, gave him a chummy grin that folded his grizzled face over on itself with wrinkles. Nick realized that the man was older than his years, probably the kind of man born old and humorless. That humorlessness probably made him a good bit of sport for the other kids on the schoolyard, making him mean and helpless, until his size caught up with him.

"Two days," Nick said. "Fine. But I need your help. Chad does, I mean."

"What's the boy want?" Chief sighed.

"He heard that Kurt DeVries, turf manager over at the club, had some illegal substance in his work locker."

Chief laughed, hard. "Let me guess, needs him locked up. Until after next Tuesday maybe?"

"Probably be long enough," Nick said. "He didn't say anything much about it."

Chief looked hard into Nick, as if trying to crack him with his gaze and make Nick spill anything he might be holding onto. "Put you on the DeVries job, huh? What do you think about that? Feel good to settle up?"

"I don't know," Nick said. "Sure."

"Sure," Chief repeated. He laughed again. Nick didn't know what to do, didn't want to set the man off but didn't want to be the butt of some unknown joke all night either.

"He'll be into work in about an hour."

"All right. All right. Sound as naggy as the missus. You probably know all about that. Oh, I'm sorry. You *did*, right? And I certainly don't mean to be disrespectful, but that's just the way I am." And the man erupted into laughter again, clutching Nick's jacket and dragging behind. He pointed to the front seat of the cruiser. Nick climbed in and Chief continued to laugh.

They drove in silence to the club. Nick dozed as the sun began to blue the black sky, then, right on time, Kurt DeVries pulled up in his brown and rusted '83 Ranger. The squeal of brakes pulled Nick from sleep and he sat straight, alert.

"Be right back," Chief said. He got out and left Nick to the county sheriff's band on the radio. Nick watched Chief walk up behind the man, towering over his short-average frame. The greeting appeared cordial. Kurt laughed before motioning with his head for Chief to come along and follow.

Nick looked around the maintenance lot, this morning like the many mornings he had come in to work. The air smelled of fresh grass clippings. The buzz of electric trimmers, weed whackers by their pitch.

Again Nick thought about that final day, his fight with Kurt, then Grete. What would she have said to him? He could never know. It was too late. Too late.

Too late.

Nick looked up as the service door opened again. It was still in the shadow of the rising sun, no sign of life.

"This is bullshit. That's what this is!"

Nick slid back to his seat as Chief marched a bleeding Kurt DeVries to the cruiser, tossing him in the backseat like a sack of potatoes. Chief got in and Nick tried to look away from Kurt, behind him, behind the metal mesh.

"Nick? Nick? What the fuck? What's this about?"

"Shut up," Chief said. "Or that little punch I gave you inside will feel like a mistress's kiss." He turned to Nick. "That's the best kind." His eyes went to the rearview. "You agree with that, Kurt?"

Kurt sat back in his seat, still a fluster of breath and blood and spit. "I don't use drugs. Never have."

"Who said you were using drugs?" Chief said.

"Not me. Didn't even think it. Marijuana these days, not really a drug in the drug sense, anyway. There's bigger problems than a stoner with the munchies. Corner one of them in an alley and they're liable to pull a microwave burrito on you!" He laughed hard at his own joke but the mood in the car wasn't uplifted any. "Okay, that isn't mine, I heard a comedian say it. But I read in the paper last summer about a black boy and guess what that son of a bitch did? Got all messed up on some bath salts he bought perfectly legally. And this is what he did: he ate another black boy's face. Believe it? No, I'm not worried about a little marijuana. We'll take care of this. Don't worry a bit." Chief laughed lightly, sounding almost jovial, but Nick saw the daggers in the eyes. Kurt stayed silent, and the rush of the road underneath the car was the only sound.

Once back in the station and safe in his cell, Kurt took on an indignant air. "I want a lawyer. Know who I was talking to the other day? Art Sokja, mayor's buddy? Sells cars? Ring a bell? This is bullshit and you know it. You'll be demoted to dog catcher when they get through with you."

Chief laughed, looked at Nick, and back to Kurt. He approached the bars, fist cocked, and Kurt flinched backward, stumbling and landing on the single metal cot against the back wall. "Think the mayor or any fucking Gyp salesman gives a shit about you? Talking to them, huh? What, while you were scraping the shit from their shoes between rounds?" Chief thumbed to Nick, "And quit looking at him; he don't have anything to do with this. And what if he did? He's going to bend my will one way and then another? Just like that? Nah, this isn't about you being a snitch, it's more than that. Just coincidence we get to do this all together. Kind of like closing a chapter on another story I suppose. Think he can guess, Kurt? Let's see. C'mon Nick, I got something interesting for you."

Nick looked at Kurt for some spark of memory or clue written on the man's face. But he just rubbed his eyes, face in hands.

Chief sat him again in the chair in front of his desk, uncuffed this time. The laptop lay closed where Chief had left it after showing Nick the video of Kimmy's confession. The Chief sifted through the mounds of papers and unmarked file folders until he found the loose gold key he was looking for. The key fit a two-drawer filing cabinet that showed much more order than the rest of the big man's work space. Meaty fingers danced over the files until he pulled the folder he wanted. Chief turned to Nick with a big smile on his broad face.

"You have a peek. I'll be back."

Nick watched Chief go and opened the folder. On top was a paper with the heading "Client Questionnaire." The information had been filled out by Penny DeVries, including all relevant contact info, spouse (Kurt) and children's names (N/A), make and model of household vehicles (Ford Ranger, Brown).

Nick had no idea what that information had to do with him but as soon as he turned the page it all became clear in a rush. He knew her body without looking at her face, the familiar birthmark on her shin. He recognized the man too, by his tattoo, barbed wire around the bicep. Nick continued flipping through the pictures, wondering how Chief managed to get such candid shots of his dead wife fucking Kurt DeVries. For a moment Nick thought that maybe they were old photos from before he and Grete were together, unlikely as that was. But that thought was quelled with the clear image of Grete's diamond ring on her finger as she clawed Kurt DeVries's back.

"Nick!" Chief called out from the small cell block. "You studied up? You ready for the test? Ha! Get your ass back here boy!"

Nick was still holding the file folder. He looked into the wide open cell. Chief was with Kurt, freshly bruised and handcuffed, holding him steady as the man stood precariously on a stack of books donated from the shelf that served as the jail "library." A bedsheet had been torn, half at Chief's feet and the other wrapped tight and tied around both Kurt's neck and some exposed pipes above. Nick looked at Kurt's arm, the barb wire tattoo poking out below the sleeve of his Rolling Hills polo.

"Everything make sense now? See Nick?"

Nick flipped through the photos again, for no other reason than to look at something different than his reality. He saw a clear picture of her face and barely recognized her for a moment. The odd expression Nick realized was a smile. This is how she used to look. A long time ago. Before the baby. The baby. And Chief asked the question at the exact moment Nick was dodging it.

"When did you break it off?" Chief said to Kurt. "'Bout the time this one's missus fell into her slump I suspect." He turned to Nick. "You know he's still married to Penny? She cried like a baby when I showed her these, but look what happened? Scared straight, huh Kurt? Or faithful anyway. What a guy. This is the part I love about public service, helping people. Saved a marriage. Got kids now too, right? Kids. Nick was going to have a kid. Knocked up his old lady, again, right around the time you ended things. That right, Nick? That about the time *you* got her with child?"

"What are you going to do to me?" Kurt said.

152

"That's up to Nick and I can't say for sure, but I suspect I know what he'll do."

And with those words Chief let go of Kurt and kicked the books out from under him. Nick watched him dangle, face red, hands fighting against the handcuffs. His toes scraped lightly across the concrete, so close to standing on his own.

"What you going to do, Nick? You want to do the right thing? Do the right thing."

"Chief," was all he could say.

"Do the right thing, Nick. You're such a helpful guy, help this son of a bitch out."

Kurt's eyes bugged out of his head. His mouth worked for words he didn't have the air to speak. His red face was turning purple.

"Do the right thing for the guy dug out your wife and put a baby in her belly. And then left the mess for you! What kind of man does that? A cowardly man is who. And a cowardly man deserves the coward's way out."

Part of Nick wanted to move. But that part was quieted again by his imagination. He wasn't walking away a good guy no matter what.

"Do the right thing." Chief grinned, gave the convulsing Kurt a swinging push. "Whee."

"You can't do this! No one's going to believe that he hung himself over some weed!"

"You're right, but if I found something else in that locker, something like pornography that depicted children? Like all the stuff I have stored in evidence? People would understand that. Probably like it better that way."

Nick saw the horror in Kurt's eyes and knew he heard the things Chief was suggesting.

"This isn't what I wanted!"

"Yes it is," Chief said. "Yes it is."

***

Chief stopped the cruiser in front of Nick's place, as Kimmy had just hours before.

"Nick, I'm not one to comfort people, but you don't need to worry about anything, you do right by me. When I saw you, when Chad asked me to scoop you up, I saw what he saw: a man devoid of purpose and full of potential. Chad pulled you in because you stepped in his circle. Now I'm yanking you out because that's what you want. You got the desire boy, but not the will. So I'm going to force will on you. You're going to like how it fits.

"You can come out as clean or dirty as you want. You want to guess who to listen to if you want out clean? Let me tell you something about me, Nick: I never hurt a woman who didn't deserve it; but I hurt every man I can, just give me the chance. So here it is, my chance. And yours if you want it. You got the reason, your life, that girl, her little one, whatever your reason it's enough. I give you the will." Chief and Nick looked at one another for just a moment. "Or I can shoot you right here."

Nick nodded and got out of the car, headed up the walk to his door.

"See if you don't feel better after you go visit that boy in Iron Mountain. You tell me you aren't in a better place. Hoo boy!"

Twelve

THE TRIP WAS six hours north of Horton and the pair got an early start. Sheldon Party Store on the edge of town was the first detour and Nick began to understand what kind of meeting it was to be when the "road snacks" included a fifth of Hennessey, a pint of peach schnapps, beers, and Dr. Peppers. He didn't know if she expected him to keep pace or if total obliteration was her game. Either way he was left to play grown up for the both of them on this journey to Iron Mountain. The quest to visit the ex-boyfriend in prison, the statutory rapist who was forever gone, excepting one hour a year Chad granted him life.

"I even went once," Chad had told him the previous evening, "first year in. Oh shit. You'll have a time. Ha!"

Nick carried the beer and a bag of corn chips to the counter. Kimmy asked for the bottles.

In the checkout a couple of guys, farm-strong in Carhartt jackets and shit kickers, started jawing at them.

"You do that to her?" one of them asked.

"I know you hear us," his friend said.

Nick turned and eyed the pair. They were bigger, best step lightly. "No."

"Sweet thing?" The first boy asked. "He do that?"

"What if he did?" she said. "Just kidding. But I have a question: Is it just you or does it smell like cow shit in here?"

Nick felt his stomach drop, a feeling he was getting used to and the realization angered him. He turned on them. "Assholes. It's her fucking business." Nick barked well and the men were taken aback. Nick paid for the booze to the sound of their muttered threats and walked out of the store with Kimmy in tow. Kimmy laughed as she followed behind fast as she could manage.

"You're going to get me killed," Nick said, and stepped into the dark lot.

"Those guys? Pfffft."

"Hey!" a familiar voice called out into the dark. The double clack cowboy footsteps hit heavy on the concrete.

"Fucking shit." Nick made for the car but gave up and spun, and caught the lead boy in the head with Kimmy's bottle of Hennessey.

"Hey!" she said, mourning her lost booze.

The lead boy dropped cold where he was hit and his partner slowed up just enough for Nick to pull the Makarov and put it in his face. The boy stopped, hands up. Nick could see that he was still a boy covered in a layer or two of baby fat.

"If you knew who she was," Nick said, "you'd want to forget us." He stepped back and dropped the weapon. Pushed Kimmy to her side of the car. "Wish I could!" he added as he climbed into the car.

"You broke my bottle!"

"I'll get you another goddamn bottle," Nick said. In the rearview Baby Face was talking into his phone, possibly taking a plate, calling for an ambulance if he was smart. Even if he called the police, he'd get Chief. Nick would like to see the big man's face upon getting the description of the assailant and his beautiful gimp.

They hit the 131 north and drove silently after another pit stop at a drive-thru liquor and porn in Reed City. Kimmy sipped on the bottle, nursing it and using a warm Dr. Pepper chaser. She passed the bottle and Nick drank. The mixture held a grip on his tongue like an intensely sweet white-trash Port. He drank again and passed the bottle back.

"I'm going to get that girl back in my arms and we are leaving this shit-forsaken cunt of a town. This place is going to die, it'll choke to death on its own cock. You watch."

"I'll pass," Nick said, reaching for one of the beers on the floor between Kimmy's feet. He faux-accidentally put the cold beer on Kimmy's thigh for a second and she squealed.

"Sorry," he said. "For snapping at you. I've known assholes like that my whole life."

"Me too," Kimmy said. "Perk of living here."

Nick cracked the can and drained half of it. He took down the rest to be rid of it and tossed the can out the window.

"What's your favorite tree?" Kimmy said.

Nick looked out the window, at the overcast black sky turning white-gray on the horizon, a thin strip between the sky and the dark expanse of pine forest. "I don't know," he said. He knew too many to pick a favorite. "I like sycamores I guess."

"Mine's the strangler fig," Kimmy said.

"Of course it is."

"What's that mean?" she frowned.

"You said it was your favorite. Set me straight."

"I just like how they reproduce. How they can just take over and smother the other tree. The old ones are hollow."

"From the dead host's rot. I know them."

"Okay, so why did you say 'of course it is?' You think I'm a parasite or something?"

He hesitated, not because it was true, which it was, but because he knew that the death that followed her was as good a reason for the association, and she didn't see it first. But there was also the innocuous beginnings of both the strangler's life cycle and their own relationship to this point. Equate a squirt of bird shit for a ride home, a dead tree robbed of its nutrients to the wonderful squeeze he was in and Nick realized he had a regular analogy. He decided not to get into all that muck.

"Death is all I mean," Nick said and left it at that. Kimmy fumbled with the radio, switched it to AM and dialed through the talk and tinny music of yesteryear. Unable to find anything, and still playing sour, she sat back with a huff.

"People think the worst of me a lot," she said. "I assume they know too much, share my insights into myself. 'Cause I think the worst of me some days.

"My mom for sure," she went on. "Bring the men in. Let 'em have their way with one of us, both. Not all of them. Some of them were nice and did the dad thing for a few weeks. Other ones just wanted someone to kick around." She laughed and looked out the window into the dark. "And I'm the rotten parent?" She took another long drink to wash down a few more valium. "I'm the one deemed unfit." Another pull from the bottle and a Dr. Pepper chaser and she was quiet. She leaned her head against the window glass and watched the scenery pass. Nick drove on. Traffic picked up as he approached the larger of the bergs in between long expanses of intermittent farmland and forest. He remembered a story he'd read for a course at State. The story was about a girl who introduced invasive species of plants and insects into the native biome. One of them was a strangler fig. Another was the tiny wasp that was the only thing in the world that could pollinate the tree. She incubated them all, hundreds of thousands of them under the nose of her biology department. Generation after generation collected and released. The birds ate the fruit and did their job. Eating and shitting fig seeds all over the forest.

But that wasn't all. The European Swallow Wort choked out life in the understory while simultaneously poisoning several small mammals, white tail fawns included. The girl in the story was a botanist trying to create a market for her particular skill set, invasive species removal and ecological rehab.

And in a way, Nick could apply the same motives to Kimmy's self-serving cynicism that guided her through life. The thought struck Nick upside the head with an unshakable bout of déjà-vu that lasted for miles and miles as they sped down the empty road. After five hours driving, the replacement bottle of Hennessey, the schnapps, and all but one of the beers, and they saw the big green sign hung over the highway: Mackinac Bridge Five Miles.

Kimmy rolled in her seat like a slippery sack of top

heavy drunk, smiling up at Nick as she slouched and slurred. "Remember that lady went over the bridge back in the eighties? My mom knew her. Or it was her cousin or something. Some shit."

"She was driving a little car like this one," Nick said. He had meant to be matter of fact, as if the scenario was some imagined hypothetical, but Nick realized he touched something in her. She sat back and said nothing as Nick drove just over the 20 mph speed limit at a strained crawl. The only sound was the rush of cool rubber meeting the road.

"I didn't mean to scare you," Nick said.

"I'm not scared. Just drive, huh?"

Nick kept his eyes on the road after she closed hers. To his right the sun was casting on gray-blue water, the waves were high, and the winds were up. Every so often a gust would give the car a little push toward the rail and Nick knew Kimmy felt it as she winced and clenched her teeth with every sway.

Off the bridge, Kimmy offered Nick the last of the bottle. He declined and she polished it off. When they pulled into the BP for gas, Kimmy went in for snacks as Nick pumped. She returned with nothing but a copy of *Barely Legal*.

She shook it in Nick's face. "Didn't have *Not Legal* so we need to make do."

Nick went inside the store. The girl behind the

counter looked bored and the few other customers were dressed in Chippewa Correctional Facility uniforms, laughing and talking at the coffee island. Nick handed money to the bored girl and she made change. He pulled out a few more bills from his pocket and dropped them on the counter. "Two packs of Kools."

He stepped out into the warm sunshine. The glow lasted till the first guard gate at the prison, where a sniffing dog was led in circles around the vehicle, IDs were demanded, intentions questioned, and questioned again, and then finally the wave-through. The road meandered wide but lazy through the expanse of facility property. A fork in the road gave them the choice of nothing and *Chippewa Correctional Facility vehicles only*.

The fork narrowed to a two-lane twist through a thick stand of pines. To the east, the trees' narrow white legs let in sunshine that painted the upslope with a trail of gold ending in a blinding eyeful of sun atop the hill. After a slow, twisting mile, the trees broke apart and the facility was before them, nested in valley, surrounded by steep hillside and trees. Not much else was around for thirty miles in any direction.

Inside there were more questions and prods. No one seemed alarmed at Kimmy's obviously drunken state, but she was quiet and upright as long as Nick supported her. The copy of *Barely Legal* was confiscated by a smiling bald man of at least seventy. He called it "general contraband" and added that for this particular convict, pornography of any kind was a specific restriction.

Five minutes after one o'clock, the fat guard led them through a series of locked doors and more security, inside to the visiting area—a surprisingly large room with few people. Twenty or so identical, square metal tables bolted to the floor with round metal stools attached. The guard left them at a table in the center of the room.

"He'll be right out," the guard said.

Kimmy was nodding off. She'd taken more pills as they left the car and Nick wondered if she'd be able to walk out of the place when their forty minutes was up. Nick looked around the room—an inmate chatted up a pair of older females, opting to lean on the table rather than sit on the small stool. A guard took notice.

"Hey. Off my table!"

The guy appeared to have not heard, but he soon slid back into the seat, level with the wet, red eyes across from him.

Tommy Witterstauter waddled with a slow shuffle that called attention as his slippers brushed against the concrete. He sat across from Nick and gave Kimmy but a passing glance as she snored on the table. His hair was shoulder length and he was clean shaven. His eyes were dusted with glittery green eye shadow and his lips were pink. On his cheek was a burn in the shape of a swastika, not an affiliation. A brand of ownership.

"Who are you?" Tommy said, his tongue poking through a hole made by missing teeth as he lifted a cigarette to his mouth.

Nick thumbed to the nearly unconscious girl next to him. "Just a ride."

"Yeah. I know. She's always got a ride. Always sleeps through the visit. I asked who you were."

"I'm nobody. I work for Chad."

"Got a name or do I call you nobody?"

"Nick."

"You going to be the one to help us, Nick?"

"How am I supposed to do that?"

The man laughed, tilting his head back and running his painted nails down the length of his smooth throat. "A fifty in my commissary is a start. Kool-Aid packets don't come cheap." Tommy pointed to his pink lips for clarification. "A girl can't get lipstick in here."

Nick nodded because he didn't know what else to do. Tommy lost it, laughing hard and eliciting a "quiet down there!" from the guard at the entrance of the visiting room. Tommy quieted and looked at

Kimmy's face for the first time.

"What happened to her face? You do that?"

Nick shook his head.

"I'm kidding. Surprised he could do that. Much as he wanted her for his. But hey, maybe that's love. It is here." Tommy began laughing again, dialing it back before the guard could holler again. Tommy lit another cigarette off the first.

"He wanted her to burn down the church in Jessup," Nick said. "She wouldn't do it."

Tommy looked at her again and smiled. He cocked his head and looked at her like a mother. "Oh, Kimmy." He wiped his eye and looked at Nick. "We were going to get married there." Tommy laughed again but the tenderness was gone. He cried lightly, looking at nothing. Another inmate walked by, put a hand on Tommy's shoulder. Tommy grabbed the hand and looked at the big black man it was attached to.

"Tonight, Ragdoll," the man said as his fingers slid from Tommy's grip.

"Tonight, baby," Tommy sniffled. He looked at Nick again and Nick saw the emptiness in his eyes, a hollowed soul staring out from the glittery green make-up. "'Ragdoll,' that's me. I didn't like it at first, but like they say, if the cock fits. And the cock that fits is the one the Peckerwoods say. That big 'ol piece just walked by, that's Whitey." Tommy laughed. "I know, right!? I'm lower than a nigger in here. They'd rather rent me to one of their enemies than protect me from them. I'm currency, man. Just a fucking sponge for all their jizz and disease. And fucking hate."

Nick didn't know what to say. It would have been comical if he didn't want to disappear. If you'd told him two weeks ago that he'd be sitting across from Kimmy Flynn's tranny ex, playing the sympathetic ear the guy waits all year for, he'd have laughed in your face. But here he was.

"Maybe when you get out? You can look her up? She still loves you."

"Ha! I got a minimum of ten to go, baby. And I ain't the same man I was."

"Who is?" Nick said. "Just try to get back somehow. You were going to marry this girl."

Tommy shook his head. "Don't talk like you know. Every time she's like this. Want to know why? It isn't the estrogen or the titties it gave me, or the make-up or even the fact that I've been passed around this place like a sex toy for seven years. You're right, Nick; I love her and I could deal with that baggage. She could. But it isn't just that. You want to know what I mean? You want to know why I just can't 'get back'?!"

Nick didn't respond. But Tommy stood up from the chair, his empty eyes burning like toxic garbage fires as he stared at Nick. "I'm going to show you. Then you'll see. Hey, maybe you can join me!"

The guard at the door hollered out, "Eighteen! Keep it civil or we'll cut you short."

Tommy looked at the guard and back to Nick, wild eyed and giddy. "Hear that? It's a big fucking joke. You want to see my big fucking joke?" And Nick could only watch as the man stood and pulled his pants down to show a shiny scarred patchwork of skin where his genitals had been. A single, dime sized plot of pubic hair remained. An equally disturbing was the text over the monstrosity, the crudely tattooed words, *No Joy*. And the sight brought with it the ghostly whiff of burning flesh and hair.

"I warned you, Eighteen! Visit over." The thick, shining black guard pulled the man away without further incident, leaving Nick to take in what he'd just seen. He looked over to Kimmy. Her eyes were glassy and she may have been smiling.

***

Nick held her hair back as she threw up in the parking lot, splashing her shoes with spittle that smelled of alcohol. She slept the entire trip back and Nick wondered if any of it had been for her benefit, if she was remembering correctly or confused, or lying. There was a man in prison on her behalf. That was something to fortify yourself against regardless of his guilt, or your own. He couldn't completely blame the girl. Face the man who made you the woman you are, or face the man you created, but why subject herself at all? Nick shook off the notion that there needed to be a reason, and for the time ignored this innate need to dig into everything. It only resulted in shit. Every time.

Nick imagined the angle for Chief. Clearly he put the man away and was interested in his release. Like Kimmy, Chief's options weren't tied into either side or even the truth. He had reason to be interested, the man, either guilty by Chief's hand or guilty by his own, it didn't matter. Chief would protect his interests on whatever side of the law they lay.

Kimmy remained passed out during the drive home. Nick drove, tunnel vision and fatigue settling in. He turned on the radio, loud for his sake, and Kimmy didn't stir. He headed south, home to Horton, to what he didn't know, but it was sure to be hell all around.

Thirteen

NICK COULD FEEL sand falling through the hourglass on his deal with Chief. He'd just given up twelve more hours and change by driving Kimmy across the state twice. Fucking Tommy. Perhaps it was the man's display in prison, but it had scared him, and, as a result, hardened Nick's resolve to do the job. Tommy was caught within the confines of the law. Innocent as his intentions, as true as they might have been to the hearts involved, law is law. The consequences were mutilated genitals, being eaten, beaten, used for profit, exploited under heavy thumbs that Horton seemed to have one too many of. As innocent as Nick wanted to be, he had to admit he was part of something his apathy couldn't rescue.

Nick's journey was in fact a quest, the oldest kind, anything available vs. the evil that threatens everything. Nick was nothing if not "anything available." It didn't matter if he liked it or not—the evil had risen up in Horton and now it needed to be slain. Which made Nick wonder why, instead of completing his deal, he was pulling into the parking garage at Ottawa Community College. He continued to wonder as he crossed the campus for Lake Huron Hall, home of the art department and campus gallery space.

Out front were the art kids. Kimmy wasn't among them. They smoked in communion around a large stone ashtray. They were the same kids—or might as well have been—that Nick went to school with at State, the community college. Nick felt as if he'd seen them all before, every day of his life. They probably knew Hobo. If they smoked, they knew Hobo.

Nick left the art kids and entered the building. He followed a series of surprisingly unartistic arrows computer-printed on white paper. As an afterthought, the word "gallery" had been written in blue ballpoint beneath each vector. As he found the service hall leading to the gallery space he heard a buzz of people and clinking glasses, voices garbled, probably behind mouthfuls of cubed cheese eaten from toothpicks. And as he entered the gallery, the scene matched his picture more or less. Cheese trays and champagne, fewer people than he'd expected. Looked like mostly the art students' parents and other acquaintances brought in by guilt or free food and drink.

Kimmy was nowhere to be seen. Nick wandered the space, looked at the various installations. Genitals were a common theme, particularly the penis. In addition to three giant plaster phalluses, one project was a series of popular children's action figures and dolls. Every figure, from The Hulk to Optimus Prime to Barbie, was equipped with an enormous and realistic looking penis.

"You like this?" a long-banged art kid asked. The kid flipped his bangs with a toss of the head and smiled. He was sweaty and smelled like he had taken a month of onion water showers in preparation for the event.

Nick signaled with a wipe of his nose that the kid had a cocaine-infused booger dangling, but the kid missed it.

"Check this out."

Cokehead Onion flipped a light switch connected to his art piece and the flaccid members on the toys began to inflate, to further exaggerated proportions. The toys began to move in unison, turning back and forth, waving the penises as music began and a chorus of tinny children's voices began singing "It's a Fucked World After All." Then the toys paired off and one animatronic toy dropped to its knees to stroke the erect cock of its partner.

Art Onion began to explain. "It's like we're infanticized, right? But at the same time, you watch TV and it's like sex and dicks and sinning and songs, and like, you want the wholesome and the dirty, right? Like you ever watch Disney Channel? And then it's like, we're all fucked anyway. You know?" The kid sniffed hard and finally wiped his nose.

"How'd you make the penises?" a faculty-looking older woman asked.

"Molded latex. I wanted to do this like on human scale and I thought I was going to get my hands on a bunch of real cocks. But that fell through. Then I was watching Disney Channel over spring break and here we are."

Nick walked away and eyed a photo series, black-and-white self-portraits complete with the obligatory cigarettes of the tortured white twenty-something. More photos, more black and white, more cigarettes, some power lines in a field of gas cans. A sculpture bust of Nicki Minaj, and in the corner, a beautiful work of oil on canvas: A Ronald McDonald presidential portrait, signature Big Mac in his hand. An apt if not stale commentary; however, the painting was not confined to the boundaries of the frame. It continued expanding from behind the bottom of the frame to include a low view of the Oval office. And behind President Ron, on all fours was the Unblessed Virgin, her face buried into the clown's fleshy butt cheeks. Her thin, bone-white fingers spread the cheeks apart as her open mouth accepted the steaming load being blown out his red asshole. And for added charm, she had also apparently just given birth to the Anti-Christ child — a perfect, horned babe. It was still connected by the yellow umbilicus, staining the presidential seal carpet with afterbirth and meconium as it screamed for the tits of its rim-jobbing mother.

Nick continued to look for Kimmy among the exhibits and installations. He made two laps around the facility and called it off, worried. A week ago he would have been thoroughly annoyed, livid, but he walked back the way he had come in with a vigilant eye in hopes of spotting Kimmy, held up by some minor inconvenience. A variety of inconveniences could have delayed her, none of them minor. Nick was afraid for her.

Any annoyance vanished when he found her sitting on the hood of his car, smoking a cigarette. She was alive and it was hard for him not to grab her and hold her just to know she was really real and they weren't in some dark Edward Hopper street corner, caught in a perfect moment surely on the cusp of some artistic perversion.

"Don't start," she said. "I'm sorry."

"What happened?" Nick said, lighting a cigarette.

She seemed confused, ready for a confrontation and having to adjust her expectations now that reality had caught up. "They wouldn't let me show my pictures. I flunked because I missed too many classes."

"You tell them you were in the hospital? Wait, photos?"

"Didn't matter. I missed too many days before all that. Yeah, my art project?"

"What about the dogs?"

She flicked that away with her cigarette butt. "That was a dumb idea. I didn't do it."

And Nick, remembering the blood and shit smell of the Parvo puppies, lugging the dogs through the field in the heat, found a reserve of the annoyance she so often tapped.

"So those dogs are just rotting in the field?"

Kimmy shrugged. "I don't know. That what dead dogs do?"

Nick didn't know how to respond but she laughed, beating him to it. He could smell the vodka that lightened her mood. No point in pursuing any of it; her absence, the dogs, and considering what had yet to be done. If he was honest with himself, he welcomed distraction from the job at hand, and Kimmy Flynn certainly was that. But as her laughter trailed off, and their friendly silence settled into the sounds of the city night around them, Nick knew that this would be the last distraction. It was time to fulfill his debt, or help the girl, or right the wrongs of the world, or shit into evil's mouth. However it would be seen when he was done and probably dead.

***

The blue light of the television flickered like the fiery thoughts licking the inside of Nick's head. Each little piece of his mess came into sharp focus before being replaced by another piece, then another and another. Chief's words in his ears, the truth about Grete and the baby. Chief was a madman, but that didn't make him wrong. Chief disappeared and Nick saw Kimmy and Chad, watched Chad beat her the night she wouldn't set the church fire. The dogs. The crows. The girl. Hobo. Nick up in bed, staring into the television but seeing nothing on-screen. He'd found something, certainly not power, not even strength or guilt. He found the little spot of light in the darkness. And that light gave him the permission to *want* to do it.

He stood in the garage doorway. His figure was backlit blackness, the light of his world spilling around him, letting the truth shine on the place of Grete's deed. The deed that had taken his child and not his child, his wife and not. After all this time it still smelled of sweet exhaust to him. He stepped to the Mustang and began clearing it of boxes of things that had accumulated. He'd moved more and more of Grete's things out of the house, usually when he'd had too many to drink, but it hadn't been to forget. It had been to send them on their way. But now the garage was a dark place where the air hung heavy with their presence, Grete's suicide sticking to them, haunting them. He left the things in the garage for whatever might be trapped there—a ludicrous thought but reasonable enough on eight lagers.

Nick booted away the rest of the personal debris surrounding the car, got in, and put the key in the ignition. He looked at the dash, his reflection against the odometer. The car had seventeen thousand miles on it. He looked up and found the garage door remote still affixed to the sun visor. Gave it a push and nothing happened. Again and nothing. Nick popped open the remote and found the brown crust of battery acid corrosion, and with a sigh Nick shuffled through the now-scattered boxes. He put a finger on the wall-mounted button but stopped as he heard the distinct clicking of glass in his house. He drew his gun and pressed his ear to the cool metal door that led back inside. Cupboards slammed. More glass. Someone was tossing his place.

Nick high-stepped it through the mess, reached another door, opened it slowly and stepped outside. He ran around the back of the house, ducking beneath windows and stopping when he'd rounded the opposite corner. He walked toward the front of the house. When he stepped around the overgrown hedge he stopped and his arms dropped. Kimmy's Volkswagen sat in the driveway, empty and the engine still ticking.

"What the hell you doing?" Nick said as he came in the front door. Kimmy was seated at the table with a bowl of cornflakes.

"Eating some cereal. Is that okay?"

Nick tucked away his gun. "What do you want? I've got something to do."

"Something for Chief or something for Chad? Or something for me?" She added the last through a fresh mouthful of cereal.

"What's the difference?"

"Don't lump me in with them. I'm stuck the same as you."

She looked hurt and Nick felt guilty. She saw that and put away her sad eyes, satisfied. She was right. And though she'd become the biggest piece of the whole Chad ordeal, she was the least responsible for Nick's tight spot. She hadn't asked for him to drive her home, so what was she supposed to do for him now? Nothing but drag them both toward their only escape. And upon thinking it through, the delayed sting hit him and Nick thought life would be better if he could turn his back on her. But he knew he was going to see this thing through with her, no more bullshit. He could sort out the rest—Kurt, Chief—later, run even. Once the job was done he could go anywhere.

"Let's go shopping," he said. And Kimmy's eyes lit up like any young lady's might.

Fourteen

KIMMY DRAGGED HER feet as she followed Nick through the aisles of Gebbins's Hardware. His plan was simple and the only way, really. Maybe too perfect, but all the pieces fell into place. He grabbed duct tape, a small hammer, and a fifty-foot heavy duty "Never-Kink" garden hose.

"Thought we were going for real shopping. Like at least to Walmart." She dragged her hand over a hanging line of paint brushes, knocking a few of them to the floor. "You one of those 'gotta support local business guys'?"

"Everything we need is here. And I can't believe you're not a little more reserved considering what we've got going."

"And what have we got? You haven't told me anything."

"You'll see. Haven't you ever heard 'show, don't tell'?"

Kimmy stopped, spun the roll of duct tape around on her finger. "No. What's that? A porno theater or something?" Then the tape flew free and into Nick's chest, bouncing into his waiting hand. He gave her a look like he'd have popped her one if he wasn't such a nice guy.

"Just playing. I know what's going on. I'm not stupid. Buy me a Coke, huh?"

***

Ten minutes and $27.16 later, they pulled int7o the parking lot of Nate's place. It was still early and the lot was empty. Nick pulled the Shelby around the side, tucking it back just beyond the view of the lot in the soft grass.

Nate was inside, wiping the bar, forever wiping the bar. Another classic Red Wings game played silently on the small TV.

"Need two screwdrivers, Nate. Drink for her, Phillips head for me." He thumbed to the door. "Can I assume you have a key to the office?"

Nate's mouth twitched. "What are you up to?"

"You really want to know?"

Nate shook his head and retrieved the screwdriver from a drawer behind the bar. He pulled the key from the nail holding up the Sokja Chevy promotional calendar featuring a different local beauty each month, each dressed in a bikini and laid out across the hood of some piece of Sokja's inventory. Kimmy had been February. And May. Nate handed over the key.

"Don't get me killed."

"I'm trying to get you alive," Nick said.

Nick went to work on the doorknob of the basement door. He carefully unscrewed, removed, reversed and replaced. He broke the key off in the lock and kicked the door shut.

"Shouldn't matter," he said. "But just in case."

"What if they notice what you did?"

Nick eyed the knob. "Let's hope they don't."

Outside, Nick grabbed the garden hose and duct tape from the car, dropping the items at the exhaust pipe. He pulled the small hammer from his jacket pocket and kneeled at a small basement window. Through the glass he saw Chad's office, half obscured by the large safe. Kimmy's safe containing the money to buy her daughter back from the State. Nick pounded a single pane of glass, hitting it tentatively at first, then smashing it with a clean strike and a shrillness that cut the ears bloody.

Nick inserted the hose into the exhaust pipe and wrapped the pair's fuck parts tight with the duct tape, winding the roll around and around, assuring no gas would escape the car except through the hose. Nick pulled the opposite end of the hose to the window, dropping it half a foot before plugging the open pane with strips of duct tape.

"Now what?" Kimmy said, placing a hand on Nick's shoulder.

Nick jumped.

"Did I scare you? I'm sorry." She laughed and tossed her hair. Nick wondered if, when she got what she wanted, she'd hit the bottle a little less. Drunk as she was now, it was a potential liability.

"You better keep it together," Nick said. "This is what you wanted. It's happening."

She moved close and he rose from the ground. She was close enough that he was obliged to take in every one of her smells, legs like honey, the summer clean smell of her laundry detergent, all the way up to her shampooed hair and vodka breath. She didn't back up, then she kissed him hard. She was determined to be a distraction but goddamn if Nick didn't kiss the girl back, tongue touching scabbed lips and finding a loose tooth. He pulled back and held her at bay as she pressed toward him.

"You're going to get me killed."

"You know you want to fuck me. Everyone wants to fuck me. Before Chad I would have fucked 'em all. Now everybody is scared to look at me." Her voice was beginning to break. "I like being looked at. I'm young still. Shouldn't I be looked at?"

"Sure. Whatever. But can we please get this done and then you can get looked at and fucked by about any guy in this town."

Harshly put, but not as harsh as her smile when he realized it was convincingly genuine. "You really think so?" she beamed.

No telling when the men would show up, so Nick wasn't surprised when he found himself stopping dead and then yanked Kimmy back by the shirt as she tried to continue past him and around the front corner of Nate's. He pressed her against the wall of the building and crept toward the corner, watched with half an eye Chad's dark-tinted black beast of a truck pull in and park.

"They're here," he whispered, and pushed her back further from the front of the building. He motioned her over to the Shelby and into the passenger seat, then waited at the doctored window for a sign of Chad's entry into death. Nick wondered how long it would take. How long for Chad and the boys to feel sleepy. Grete was dead in under a quarter hour. Fifteen minutes from bliss and heaven. Then he remembered Kurt, tried to imagine that kind of pain—a special pain akin to what a guy might face in a burning highrise as fire moved in, licking closer. He thought about how Grete chose death over him. Death for the right man was better than life with the wrong one, and the bondage a child shackles onto a couple? Nick wondered what it was like to care that deeply/be that off balance as to make someone choose their own end, defy biological imperative. Nick cared about nothing that much. Perhaps there was hidden value in apathy.

Nick shook it away. Useless, wasted energy. Voices came from inside the office. Laughter and the clinking of glasses. If they were in this early it was to talk business, plan, see how the window-smashing business was working out. Nick figured he had an hour before they'd come up for air on their own, and considering he had three grown men and two dogs to deal with, he was going to need most of that hour.

Nick slid into the driver's seat and put his hand to the key. This wasn't like letting Kurt die. This was his baby. He'd planned this, every detail. And at the moment, there was no passion to force his hand, only the usual forces, like the one sitting next to him, willing him to turn the key. He could feel it the same as the heat of her breath on his neck as she leaned in.

"I'm sorry I put you here."

The engine of the Shelby rumbled to life.

***

The silence was too much after only five minutes. Nick turned on the radio, punched at the station buttons, stopped on an ad for Sokja Chevy—the one where he talks about firing midgets out of a cannon. They were actually dwarves and Art must have known that. But he never changed anything when he reshot the same ad every year for the August Auto Blowout event.

"He really shoot those midgets, you think?" Kimmy asked.

"I know he does. I mean, he doesn't do it. They're professionals. Circus act. You've never seen it?"

"No."

"They're good." Nick looked out all the windows again, checking for any sign of detection, mapping out an escape for the minute this all went south. "Don't want this shit backing up on us," he said, opening the window. The sun was setting and the occasional car headlight brushed across their field of view, never quite touching them. Maybe that was why Nick began to let himself think he might get through the night without a bullet in his head or ripped apart by dogs. Kimmy played with the dials, stopping on an oldies station. Steel guitars gave a woozy, wavy voice to the gas he was pumping into Nate's basement. They both looked out the windshield at the pink sun.

"Can I ask you something?" Kimmy said.

"My permission never stopped you before."

"Do you miss your wife?"

It was a question he wouldn't have known how to

answer the day before. "I did. Sometimes, but, it wasn't a marriage for quite some time." Nick shifted and checked the rearview for signs of activity. "Less so than I ever thought it turns out."

"How's that?"

"She killed herself over a man. Killed herself and the unborn baby. His, it turns out."

"Oh," Kimmy said. Nick waited, wondered what that brain of hers was going to process his words into, where they might take her own thoughts. "I could never hurt my baby."

Nick wanted to tell her that she was already hurt by having her mother taken away, by being left with a relative who, by her own accounts, wasn't fit...By giving her life in the first place. But he didn't say that.

"I think most people would say the same thing. She didn't talk to me. I thought it was some kind of pregnancy blues. Never would go see anyone. Said she didn't want to take any pills, and that's all the doctors were good for. So we rarely spoke until the day she did it. And then less. Obviously."

"'Kay," Kimmy said.

"You miss Tommy?"

"Every day," Kimmy said. She opened her mouth to continue but the words didn't come, wouldn't. Maybe it was something she was too young to be ready for, losing everything important, leaving her as confused and lonely as her little girl.

They watched the sun, and as the last of it fell below the horizon, he felt her hand on his. He turned his palm up and she gripped his hand tight. "You're a good man. I don't know if I ever met one. Not since Tommy."

Nick laughed lightly. "'Good man' in your book is one who'll kill for you."

Kimmy thought about that a moment and squeezed his hand, smiled. "If that happens to be what I most need…Friends do for friends. If it comes from good, it's good."

Where did he come from? Nick checked his watch as the sun finally dipped completely from view. "It's about time," he said. He killed the engine.

Nick and Kimmy walked through the dark lot and into Nate's place and he nearly took her hand, old habits and new feelings being what they were. As soon as they stepped through the door he was grateful that he hadn't acted on the impulse. The usual crowd was there, shooting pool, throwing darts, drinking. Nick stopped dead when he saw Chad hunched over the bar on Nick's stool—the dogs resting alert on the floor. Nick stood dumb, wanted to run before Chad saw him, but it was futile.

"There they are," Chad said loudly without looking from his bottle. "Here's the love birds."

With no other option, Nick stepped forward and Kimmy followed. She passed Nick by and threw her arms around Chad's neck.

"What the heck you talking 'bout, baby?"

Chad's eyes went from Nick to Kimmy and his eyes took on a default gaze, one that could go either way depending on the answers he received. But when his eyes found Nick again, they had the only answer they wanted.

"Git the fuck off me, cunt."

Kimmy stepped back. "Baby?"

"Don't 'baby' me! Don't! You think I'm a fucking idiot? You know I didn't mind you playing buddy with this boy, having him around for all the bitch work. I thought maybe he was a fucking homo, or at least had some sense about him." He turned to Nick. "What'd I tell you, Gillis? What the fuck did I tell you about Uncle Kurt? Remember?"

"I do," Nick said. "But it isn't like that. Not at all."

"Ha. Not 'at all.' But it is *at some*."

Nick felt the weight of the Makarov in his pants, looked at the dogs and wondered if he could land two head shots before Chad could whip out whatever he was carrying. But the hounds found his gaze and stood alert, rumbling low and licking their muzzles. Chad turned back to his drink and had he wanted, Nick could have pulled the gun. But he didn't. The clacking billiard balls and curious eyes kept him frozen. Chad poured another shot. "Set me up with two more, Nate."

Nate didn't flinch. He pulled out two more glasses and poured a shot of Maker's into each before filling Chad's once more.

"Drink up," Chad said. Nick and Kimmy took their shots in hand and drank. Chad looked at them, smiling sickly through glassy eyes that might have been confused for tears. "Hope you enjoyed it. Now both of you...get downstairs. Erik and Russell are waiting. Move it!"

Nick was first down the stairs, not sure of what he'd find and not sure of what would happen when he found it. Couldn't be good no matter what. Chad shoved Nick through the door and into the office.

"We're here, boys!" Chad announced. But Erik and Russell didn't respond. "I said no drinking 'til this was done! Wake the fuck up!" But the men couldn't wake up, peaceful as they appeared.

Chad moved past Nick with a shove and looked at his boys. The fact they were dead clicked and he spun around. Nick felt the awful heat in his gaze, white hot.

"You? You did it!" Chad shouted as a few of the pieces, the important ones, fell into place. "Oh no, motherfuckers! Git 'em!"

Nick heard the words and they seemed to slow as they came out of Chad's mouth, hanging in the air between the ears of each concerned. And when the words finally found the dogs, everything began to move much too quickly. The words triggered the release of that steadfast aggression that was always, always bubbling just under the surface of these pups. Nick saw Hobo. Then he only saw what was in front of him as the dogs sprang forward. Nick did the only thing he could, running from the office, feeling the tight squeeze-toothed vice around his calf as he reached the door separating the room from the stairwell. Nick yelled, lurching forward, and backhanding the door into the face of the second dog. His leg still in the grip of the first, he slammed the office door on the dog's giant head—at first to no effect—but Nick slammed again and again and finally the beast had had enough, relented momentarily with a squeal and released Nick. His momentum nearly sent him sprawling to the landing, but Nick caught himself on the stairs. He scrambled up them and both dogs, after fighting for the narrow space between the partially closed door and jamb, were on his heels.

Nick emerged from the stairwell a madman, leaping from the top step to the top of Nate's clean bar. Somewhere he heard a scream, then the sound of hard claws on the wooden floor. Nick scrambled down the length of the bar and hit the door with full force, spilling from the furnace and into the cool night air. He fell back against the door, tried to hold it shut against the dogs' force, but the door wouldn't latch. He pushed himself from the door and made a dash for the Shelby as he pulled his piece. Then took a quick peek behind, pointed and fired.

The yelp was the only way Nick knew he'd hit something. He rounded the corner and felt the relief of seeing the car at the exact moment he felt the hard clamping jaws on his already damaged leg. He hit the ground face first, got a mouthful of gravel and dropped the Makarov. He rolled over, tasted blood in his mouth. The beast let go of his leg, its jaws dripping with blood and saliva. Behind it, the other hound limped ahead, its left front leg useless. The unbroken dog met Nick's eyes and lunged for his face. Nick grabbed the dog's collar and held it up on its hind legs while the chomping jaws opened and closed in a frenzied pursuit. The wounded animal caught up and prepared to sink its teeth into Nick's bad leg. Nick swung the leg, kicked the dog's shattered limb. It retreated slightly with another screaming yelp. The dog in Nick's hands continued to chomp and press forward. Nick strained against the beast, sheer will and adrenaline the only things keeping him out of the wild jaws. Nick brought his legs underneath and used his knees to support the bulk of its weight. He let go of the collar with his right hand and punched the dog hard and square in its huge black nose. The animal squealed like the first and doubled back, pawing at its throbbing snout. Nick scrambled to the car, the dogs still coming, but slowed slightly by a hint of caution. Nick slammed the door of the Shelby as both dogs jumped against the window, their full fury had returned as they realized they'd failed their master. The jaws snapped and wet muzzles spread blood and slobber on the glass. Nick watched the wounded dog's forelimb hanging limp by a flap of skin, the white bone showing like jagged teeth popping through bleeding gums. Nick laughed loudly, mocking the dogs with his dry, cracked scream.

"Fuck you!" he said flipping double birds. "FUUUUUUCK YOOOOOUUUUU!"

Nick turned the key and brought the engine to life. He shifted into gear and stepped on the gas, tires spinning and tearing at grass as the Shelby pulled away. Nick hit the lot and swerved left as a young couple jumped out of his path. In his rearview he saw the dogs, still pursuing, as Chad stepped out the front door of Nate's, dragging Kimmy behind him. The whole scene receded in the rearview as the car left the lot. The garden hose dragged behind with the soft ping of its metal threads. The one dog gave chase, but it too disappeared with everything else. Nick looked at his face in the mirror, spattered with dog drool and his own blood. His heartbeat began to slow, and he took note. It wasn't real. A false calm came over him, and though out of immediate danger, he knew there would be more blood. Much more. Likely some of it would be his.

Fifteen

NICK DITCHED THE Shelby in the Horton High School parking lot and crossed the grassy football practice field, climbed the hill beyond and hopped the fence surrounding the playground of the adjacent South Elementary. The place was dark except for the spotlight affixed to the corner of the red brick building. Nick followed the sound of a rhythmic metal-on-metal scream and found that white-haired Bizbang kid swinging alone in the dark, staring at him as he approached.

"Hey," Nick said. Unable to ignore the gaze and that white mop of tangled hair.

"Wanna see me jump off the swing?" the kid said.

"No. I'm busy."

The kid launched himself from his seat and flew in front of Nick and into the wood-chip-covered playground. That's when Nick saw the boy wasn't alone, but with a pair of dark twin boys around his age. The pair sat on the jungle gym staring at Nick like twin birds, vultures or crows. Neither spoke or moved except to pass a jar of rubber cement between them.

"You see that?" the Bizbang kid said. "I went like a hundred feet!"

"Yep. That's great, kid," Nick said.

The kid jumped at his heels like a dog. "Want to see me slide down the slide on my feet?"

Nick regretted having spoken to the kid. "No. I told you I'm busy." He spotted a slide across the playground. "Wait. Yeah. Go do that."

The kid ran off and Nick continued away from the school and toward Allen Street.

"Hey!" he heard the kid yell from the top of the slide. "You aren't watching!"

Nick kept moving and listened to the sound of rubber on wet metal then a significant ringing thud. He didn't turn around, just kept walking. He knew where he was going. He didn't want to go there, but he was out of options. It wasn't too late to run. He should. But when he thought of Kimmy getting the totality of the beating meant for him...she was probably dead already, but that couldn't cut him from the tether she had on him. No matter how she came into his life, whose fault it was, she was in it, and she was the first person he'd wanted anything for in a long time: he wanted her safe. He wanted her to get the money. He wanted her with her child.

And that was the only reason he could piece together for finding himself on the steps of the

Horton Police Department again, bleeding up the stone stairs to find Chief waiting for him behind the glass door. Chief stepped out to meet him, but it wasn't cordial.

"You fucked up, didn't you?" Chief grabbed him by the throat, and as Nick began to choke, he saw in Chief's gray eyes the reflection of every other man who'd feared for their life while in his grip. His hand went to his back, but his piece wasn't there.

"He's got Kimmy," Nick choked out. "Let me finish it."

Chief's gaze was rock hard and he squeezed tighter before letting go and shoving Nick aside. Nick stumbled and choked. He dropped to his knees for breath and Chief descended the stairs in front of him.

"I know he's got her. I was waiting for you. Now get in the car."

Nick pulled himself to his feet, still coughing. "Where we going?"

"He wants you delivered. Called me right after. Says bring you in if I see you."

Nick almost asked where exactly he was getting delivered *to*, but he already had an idea. The blonde girl, tucked away to rot under sterile dirt. Nick saw it clearly, so he sat back and kept his mouth shut. Chief drove them south, out of his jurisdiction, where he wouldn't pretend he was upholding any kind of law.

Nick didn't know what kind of trip this was going to be. Chief hadn't killed him, though his eyes had said he'd wanted to. Nick must still be worth something to the man.

Nick felt Chief's eyes on him in the dark. "What?" he said.

"You really shoot his dog?"

"Yeah," Nick said.

"No talk is going to save you. He loves those dogs."

"Doesn't matter what I do. I fucked his goat," Nick said.

Nick looked at Chief. The man looked straight forward, a puzzled look on his face before turning back to Nick.

"What's that now?"

Nick shook his head and looked out his window, head against the cool glass. On the side of the road was a deer, car-struck and mangled. Nick guessed it was a buck since someone had gone to the trouble to cut off the head. It would go up on someone's wall and they'd tell the story about hunting it down, never mentioning that the weapon was their car. Nick wondered what kind of stories would be told when whoever did him in admired his own head on their wall. The whole idea brought Nick to laughter—his head on the wall for posterity—a legacy as the example of someone who'd made bad choices. Still, it was a legacy.

"So funny?" Chief said.

"Death."

Chief pulled out a half pint of Maker's from under his seat. He killed the bottle and threw it from the cruiser, shattering it. "You got that right," he said, drawing his sleeve across his wet mouth.

***

Nick was about to tell Chief to slow down or he'd miss the hidden drive, but the man did it on his own. The summer corn slapped at the vehicle like the first time Nick visited the property with Kimmy. The cruiser emerged from the corn and lit up the dark house Kimmy grew up in. Chad's truck was there too, sitting empty, as dark as everything else. Nick watched Chief check out the vehicle and pulled out his phone.

"Got him," he said. He waited as the person on the other end spoke. "Yeah, we're here." Chief looked at Nick. "Where? He does? All right then. Be there directly." Chief put the phone away and turned again to Nick. "He says you know where to go. So go."

Nick headed into the corn, still unsure where any of this was going, but now considering the fact that his failure to take care of Chad was enough reason for

Chief to sell him out. Unless, maybe, if he did the job. But he was without the Makarov and Chad surely had his gun, and at least one dog still capable of tearing him apart. His legs felt like they were made of broken glass pieced back together with jelly. But he walked on because there was nothing else he could do. Of course he could get lost in the corn, but how long could he stay there before he was found? And if he wasn't found, where would he go? He wished for a riverboat like they'd stolen the night they delivered the cow. The mystery fate of a stolen piece of livestock was preferable to the things running through his mind.

They walked on, taking the familiar turns he knew well from carrying the coins and the dead dogs. Everything seemed a lifetime ago as he stepped into the clearing beyond the corn, splashing through the creek and up again, toward another clearing and what waited there.

"Made it," Chad said. A campfire blazed behind him. Kimmy sat on a stump holding her hands up to the fire as if to warm them, though the evening wasn't cold. Chad caught Nick's gaze. "Don't look at her. She doesn't need nothing from you. Nothing you got to give her."

"Are you all right?" Nick called past Chad. Kimmy didn't say a word, flipped her wrists and baked the backs of her hands.

"Don't TALK to her! You talked enough. Been talking about bad things." Chad looked at Chief. "Criminal things."

Chad looked back and forth from Nick to Chief, waiting for the bigger man to speak.

"What do you want me to do?" Chief said. "Here he is. He's your problem."

Nick noticed the dogs. The one Nick had shot lay behind Chad, licking and chewing at its mangled leg. The dog Nick had punched sat at the ready by Chad's side, its bruised nose painfully aware of Nick's scent. The dog rumbled low when Nick found its black eyes. Neither would look away.

"Easy," Chad said to the dog. "My problem. Should have taken care of you from the git. Sure Erik and Russell would have appreciated it.

"You fooled me, Nick. I thought you were one of the good ones. Only wish those other boys were here to watch you die."

Kimmy was still at the fire, listening to the men speak, but hugging herself and staring into the flames.

"I never wanted this. I wish Hobo was here. You took from me first. I'm not asking for anything but a pass to move on. I'm willing to let it all go."

Chad scratched the ears of his dog. "I'm sure you are. Now that I got you. But what about when you were plotting against me? What about that? Justified in anybody's mind or not, I can't have that. The only thing you got going for you, Nick, is that you have my money. I'll give you the gift of a bullet. Dogs will eat either way. But you don't have to watch them eat is what I'm saying."

"I don't have it," Nick said.

"Say again?"

"Said I don't have it."

"This is it. Three times you going to deny me?"

Nick looked at the girl. Something shone bright against her lips, reflecting silver and stars back to the fire. "I don't have your money, Chad."

Chad gave the look. Shook his head and this time there was something else in his eyes; it was sadness, true sadness and loss.

"Thought we was going to be buddies, Nick. You hurt me bad, friend. You say you don't have the money, okay. Maybe you don't. You made your choice." Chad smiled and knelt beside his animal. He unclasped the leash from the collar and didn't have to command the dog to attack. The dog wanted to taste Nick again. And as the dog hit him, its giant paws knocked the wind out of him and put the sharpest screeching ring in his ears. He fought, the dog chomping down on a forearm. Nick punched at the dog's thick skull as it shook him in its jaws. The piercing shriek stabbed his eardrums again. He hit the dog again, strength waning. He couldn't hold the dog any longer. Nothing but black before his eyes.

And then he was free.

Nick sat up in the dirt, the fire smoke blowing in his face and burning his eyes. The dog was gone but for its howling, painful and desperate. Nick watched as one of the beasts burst from the dark, snarling and yelping as it was seemingly swallowed up again by the blackness it had just escaped.

Nick looked away and found Kimmy, his angel lit in flame, the silver whistle now silent between her lips. In the light of the flame Nick could see the crows, descending on the scene from all sides, collecting over two distinct, howling mounds. Chad ran from mound to mound, shooing the birds to no avail, getting bitten, bleeding knuckles for his trouble. And the birds kept coming, joining the piles, tearing apart the dogs.

Nick watched as Chad stood between his silent guards, hands bloody with beak wounds. He kicked at the piles, injured some birds but not nearly enough to matter, as any piece of the dog that became open to pecking was quickly filled by another crow. Nick looked to Chief. The big man seemed surprised, amused even. And Nick watched him shift his gaze to Kimmy as she stood from her seat at the fire, whistle still between her teeth, face dusted with soot. Dangling from her hand was a small plastic bucket Nick had seen before. With her free hand she threw handfuls of corn, and the birds descended on it. The forgotten dogs were pecked to death, eyes gone, nearly skinned, entrails exposed, their blood soaking into the soil.

"What the fuck did you do?" Chad screamed. He stepped toward her and slapped her hard across the face, dropping her like a rock into the sterile earth. Nick sprung to his feet but he felt the big man's hand on his shoulder, pushing him back to the ground. Chief stepped past him, his size fourteens kicking up puffs of dust.

Nick watched Chief blow in like a storm. Chad turned from Kimmy and his eyes, glassy and wide, found Chief. They showed no sign of fear. Nick wondered if he'd forgotten his dogs were just eaten by crows.

Chad threw a fist into Chief's face, followed up with two more that did little to slow the man. As the big man pressed, Nick watched Chad's face change, his eyes losing something, trading in their confidence for a fear Chad hadn't felt in a very long time, but in Nick's eyes, it appeared to be a fear that suited him, a fear that was real, and maybe worst of all, a fear that was warranted.

Chief grabbed Chad by the front of the shirt and whipped out his baton to length with a crack. Chad threw a few more shots that Chief ignored as he began to work on the boy's legs, making Nick wince with each blow as Chief brought the King of Horton to his knees.

Chad rolled in the dust, tried to stand, got a baton across the jaw for his trouble. It dislocated the mandible from the rest of the skull. The broken bone hung loose and blood spilled from Chad's mouth. Satisfied with the result, Chief let out a laugh and went back to work on the legs, breaking any bones foolish enough to try and defend.

Chief stopped and Nick watched the man, his barrel chest heaving, a smile on his face, tears. Chad moaned and Nick dared not speak. But his mind was screaming, telling him to *run run run*. And he nearly did until Chief went back to work on Chad, and Nick was planted in place, not by fear, but incredulity. The brief respite had invigorated Chief and he continued to rain down on his target. Chad screamed garbled pleas and prayers. "Shut up, you fuck. I'm your fucking God." Chief started on the ribs and a few cracks silenced the screams to whimpers. Then it was the arms. Chad didn't struggle, not a sound He lay with the fear of God draining from his mangled mouth. Nick watched tears fall from Chad's eyes to the dirt and mix with the blood.

Chief looked as peaceful as Nick had ever seen him, circling the living corpse, using his hard steel toe to prod and elicit a wincing squeal. And then the big man was done. Chief circled the broken boy, admired the handiwork, smiled as he kicked dirt into Chad's eyes.

Chief snatched the boy by the front of his jacket like he was nothing. Chad's screams were now bahhing like sheep, a single vowel spat through more blood. Chief dragged him like a limp doll and delivered him to the coin vault, dropped him at the dugout doorway before jumping into the hole and shoving the boy through with his foot. He stuffed him into the pit, made the broken boy fit, stuffing and folding the broken form through the too small a hole, like a ragdoll into a dollhouse that wasn't quite large enough

Kimmy stepped to the hole and looked in on the broken man who'd once broken her. She said nothing. But her hand did find Chief's. She squeezed it slightly just a moment before releasing. She turned to Nick, finally getting his own ass out of the dirt.

"Let's go get the money, I guess," she said. And she left Chief and Nick to follow. Chief pointed Nick to the field with a sharp nod toward the corn.

Nick watched Kimmy as she stared at the house

she grew up in. It wasn't a home, he could see in her eyes. He thought about the scarecrow man, now dickless with an asshole like a paper towel core, just one of the many men that had rolled out of her mother's bed. Maybe it had been him, maybe it hadn't. But it didn't matter, right one wrong one, all the same. Nick saw it written on her face. She reached for Nick's hand and pulled him behind her.

"Let's scoop up that money, huh?"

***

The haul was a lot heavier than fifteen thousand dollars, closer to twenty-four, which in theory made for a nice three-way split. The three parties looked into the trunk of the car, at the pile of bill bundles so nice and neat in the C and C Windows duffle bag. Chief reached out and closed the trunk hard.

"Girl," Chief said. "Take his car back to the bar. Nick and I have one thing to take care of."

Nick and Kimmy looked at each other and Nick remembered Kurt in the cell. He nodded to Kimmy and she took his keys and called him to the driver's side.

She pulled him close, friendly, and hugged him. "You're a good one, Nick. You never wanted any of it I know. But take your cut when you're done with whatever you're doing and get out of here. Find something you can do for you."

"What if I wanted to stay?" Nick said.

She laughed. "Nobody wants that. And Nick didn't know if she meant no one in Horton wanted to stay there, or if no one wanted *him* to stay in Horton. And he had to admit, it stung a bit, the town's rejection of him.

"Good luck with your kid," Nick said.

"Should be painless. Like everything, right?" She smiled. She opened the door to get into Nick's car, the car he'd used in his idiotic attempt to pull his wife out of her funk. She turned back to him. "He was lying. I never asked him to hurt my man. I just wanted him scared." She laughed again. "That's the thing about being so pretty in a town like this, everyone overdoes it."

"You can't overdo anything," Nick said. "You can only do it."

"You know who you sound like?" she said.

"Yeah," Nick said. "I do."

Nick took a moment to linger on her face. It was healing, but her left eye drooped and the scar across her broken nose was still angry.

"I'll leave your cut at Nate's. Thank you." She turned to the girl she'd pulled from the house in the night, the girl who was still sleepy, waiting for her mama in the car. "Say goodbye to the only good man I ever met."

"Bye," the child said and put her head onto her mama's shoulder.

Nick waved her off as she drove away. He knew that she wouldn't be at Nate's when he got there: his money and car, but not her. And he remembered what she said, about nobody wanting to stay in Horton. She was no exception and she was a smart girl who knew an out when she saw it coming. Knew one when she saw *him* coming.

"Let's go, Nick."

He got into the front seat of the cruiser, deflated in the seat, exhausted, no more energy to spend on hope or sorrow or fear or revenge—his own or anyone else's.

Sixteen

CHIEF OPENED THE station's door, let Nick in first. Nick heard the click of the lock behind him. Chief pulled him through the lobby and into the guts of the station, which wasn't much but Chief's small, paper-strewn office and a pisser. They walked through the heavy metal door that led to the small cell block. Kurt was still hanging from his cell, hands loose at his sides, a clear suicide.

"What?" Nick said.

"Get rid of him."

Nick laughed, emboldened by exhaustion. "Fuck that! This is your mess."

"And you were going to take care of the other mess for me so I didn't have to. Best laid plans, yes? But that ain't worth a sack of sand here."

Nick looked at the body. "Is this it?"

"It's it when I say it's it."

"Like hell it is. I'm done. I'm gone."

Chief stared at him, smiled at Nick as if he were a child protesting bedtime. And in his smile Nick remembered the tape.

"You made me a promise, Nick. You didn't come

through. You were supposed to take care of that boy. You failed to deliver. You expect me to do my part? Contract is null and breached by both parties. What's left to do but renegotiate?"

Nick looked into the cell.

Do the right thing.

He saw Kurt fighting again, freshly dropped, flailing his legs, fighting the good fight against the handcuffs. It was instinct to fight at the end. To the end. Even if Kurt's end was a false charge to keep him from a league match that wasn't going to happen. He wasn't supposed to die. But a lot of things happen to people that aren't supposed to.

"Kimmy won't go through with it. She'll tell them what really happened. Chad's gone. She's on her own."

"She won't need to. She'll be gone."

"I won't let you," was as far as Nick got before Chief whipped him upside the head with an open palm that rang Nick's bell and dropped him to a dizzy knee.

"Why would I hurt her? I say I can make her gone. I mean the good kind of gone. Girl's the only good thing I ever made." Nick looked up into his steel gray eyes and watched them read his mind.

"She doesn't know," Chief said. "And she doesn't need to. Not without complications, to be sure, but sometimes it works out, like it did tonight. You get a chance to love your child, get a chance to be the kind of man your girl needs. I thought it was taken care of when we put Tommy away, but Chad, well, you saw his handiwork, sucked you right in. You know what I mean, what it's like to want to protect something."

He did. Nick also knew what it was like to chase after a single failure, to know what it was and to know that he'd have to see it in every pretty girl's face for the rest of his life. And it was this trait that once again directed him, made him think of Kimmy, made him speak for her well-being. "So tell her," Nick said. "Don't you want her to know if she's so valuable to you? Shouldn't she know you? Be a grandfather and just leave me out of it!"

"I do know her, Nick. I know her as much as I can. I'm a man doesn't do well with others all the time. Small doses is how I like my people.

"She doesn't need to know me. She's got what's good of me and that's enough for both of us. For all of us."

Nick looked at Kurt's body. "Who's 'all of us?'"

"I got critters all over town! Funny how many times I get a call to check out a lonely lady's 'bump in the night.' Always the same, first they offer coffee. At midnight. Ha!"

Nick stood silent. All over town there were little

Chiefs, pretty girls and boys sure to grow up big and strong. Nick again looked to Kurt.

"Where do you want him?"

"You know where, but we got to do something first. Raise your right hand."

Nick did. "Why?"

Chief put a hand on Nick's shoulder, squeezed it affectionately before bearing down and gripping like a pair of jaws, smiling the whole time. "I need a new deputy. Let's get you sworn in."

Seventeen

NICK STEPPED OUT of the pink trailer home in his freshly pressed police uniform. Chief had been good as his word and put Nick to work, on the city's dime, no less, into the new sunshine. It was a cool morning, but the weather report promised a real scorcher. Best time to start his duties was now.

All the way back to the property, Nick pondered the idea of choice as presented to him by Chad Toll, the dead man still a ghost in his ear. Chad was right about choice, generally, but he was wrong specifically. No one has one choice in any situation. Truth was, Nick knew he had an infinite number. And fact was, in Nick's mind, most folks went with the easy choice. Went with it so often it became habit. Or maybe a rut.

Nick did like the Chief asked. Kimmy's mama moved out of the little house and into a condo community north of Horton. Nick moved in to maintain the property and do the odd jobs his new position as deputy required. His own house in Horton sat empty, but for the time being that had to be better. That wasn't his house. Nick wondered if it ever was his after Grete was gone. He'd thought of her as a ghost haunting the place, but in hindsight, maybe it was him doing the haunting. He laughed to himself as he stepped off the porch of the old Flynn place and into the yard.

The birds began to gather as Nick approached the shed. Several perched on the vending machine that had been sitting silent since they last emptied it of corn, the day Kimmy had shown him only a glimpse of what the birds where capable of. Nick filled the corn bucket, tossing handfuls into the yard, watching the birds descend on the meal. In the distance came the sound of the thresher, a thin string of diesel exhaust plumed as the machine chomped on corn acres away. Soon the field would be cut for the season, its comforting shade gone for another year. Nick held his breath and stepped into the corn.

At the clearing, Nick took a handful of corn from the bucket and threw it over his shoulder. He heard the strangely soothing flapping of wings and the sound prodded him forward as he stepped into the hole, crouched down and gripped the particle board door, pulled the wood free and set it above ground.

Inside the pit, Chad squinted against the invading light. Behind him, his blonde continued to stink and rot. Nick watched him tentatively move a broken arm, hoping to shield the sun. Chad winced and shut his eyes. "Nick? Is that you, Nick? Get me out of here,

Nick. I need to get to the hospital! Please Nick. I'm going to die in here! Help me."

"I don't know what the fuck you're trying to tell me with that mangled mouth of yours but you may as well shut up. Chief told me to feed you and that's what I'm here to do." Nick tossed the bucket of corn into the hole, shutting Chad in to scream himself stupid, but never dead.

Nick tried to tune out the screams, which were only slightly muffled when the wooden door was back in place. He wished he'd been able to leave the corn without rousing Chad. He wished he'd found the man dead so he could shut the underground cell away forever, listen to the sound of falling dirt instead of the screaming that just wouldn't stop. And as nice as the thought was, Nick found himself submitting to the sound, forcing himself to listen, to not ignore the screams that that followed him back into the corn. He listened because they were never going away. He knew that now. And what could he do about it? Nothing. Not a god damned thing. There was nothing left for him to do but sit in his shining new police cruiser, start the engine, and continue to listen.

About the Author

CS DeWildt is the author *of Love You to a Pulp, Candy and Cigarettes, The Louisville Problem, and Dead Animals*. He lives and writes in Tucson, Arizona. He is currently working on a new novel.

Acknowledgements

I want to specifically thank the following people for their continued support:

Kimmy Dee
Heath Lowrence
Mary Alles
Dan VanderKooi
S.W. Lauden
Brian and Lindsey Hullfish
Richie Lampani & Rocket Lounge
Elaine Ashe
David S. Atkinson
Josh Martin
Bryan Wells
Pat & Heather Brazee
David S. Atkinson
Bill Baber
Jim DeKorne & Julianne Bergstrom

And a very special thank you to my 2 AM secret weapon, 5-Hour Energy.

More from All Due Respect Books

We hope you enjoyed Kill 'Em with Kindness. *Below are a few of our other recent releases. For all of our crime fiction titles, check us out at allduerespectbooks.com*

VERN IN THE HEAT
By Rob Pierce

Vern is a dangerous man—he makes illegal exchanges safe. Until someone tries to rip off a drug deal he's working and he gets blamed. Now both gangs involved are after him, including the one he works for. And he's going to clear his name, no matter who he has to kill in the process.

DEBT CRUSHER
By Michael D. Pool

Cam Reynolds has a problem. When Cam's longtime boss Tom Colcetti dies and leaves control of his criminal organization to his predatory son Tommy, Cam may finally get the chance to run a crew of his own. But Tommy has his eyes on new business horizons, and Cam just made a mistake that could destroy Tommy's heavy-hitting new partnership. Now Cam must struggle against violent forces of betrayal, lust, and greed as he attempts to either salvage his career, or get out of the game with his life still intact.

SQUEEZE
By Chris Rhatigan

Scumbag newspaper reporter Lionel Kaspar aimlessly wanders from one scam to the next. Trying to claw his way to anywhere, Kaspar fabricates news stories and blackmails a local bureaucrat. What little success Kaspar stumbles upon he wastes betting on sports and drinking. But when Greg Hulas, his competitor, starts investigating him, Kaspar becomes desperate to maintain his position.

Made in the USA
Lexington, KY
20 June 2016